NOW IT SEEMS THAT I'M NOT HERE AT ALL

STORIES

SUZANNE BURNS

TAILWINDS PRESS

Tailwinds Press
P.O. Box 2283, Radio City Station
New York, NY 10101-2283
www.tailwindspress.com

Published in the United States of America
ISBN: 979-8-9853124-4-7
1st ed. 2023

Now It Seems That I'm Not Here at All

CONTENTS

THE AFFAIR

Fruit weighted the car from the tourist orchard to the motel at the edge of town. Apples mostly, with names almost too exotic to believe. Glass Slipper, Lady Rose, Orange Plush, Black Beauty. Leonard unloaded the bounty of bushels and pecks into their room, plastic bags stamped in words from a nursery rhyme Constance once loved to hear her mom sing as she pushed her on the backyard swing. Bushels, pecks, hugs around necks. A peck of Black Beauties cost five dollars, a bushel of Lady Roses, ten.

"What are we going to do with all of these?" Leonard's breath caught in his throat, almost like something held him down, she thought, gripped him around the neck like she sometimes fantasized doing on evenings like this, ruining their adventure with his unmistakable Leonard tone.

Like that one time they stayed up an hour later on a work night to watch a scary movie. The one about the devil child and Gregory Peck. Still handsome, those dark eyebrows, that career in British politics. Still devilish after forty-five years, this devil child. Still dead from cancer, the movie wife with the movie skin you could almost see through. It was all Constance thought about as the devil revealed himself, how the seed of cancer could hide in someone so lovely, those icy eyes, that paperwhite petal skin. The thought of the actress' death took her out of the movie until her gourmet popcorn brought her back. The truffle salt. The walnut oil. The near-hand-holding as the couple fished for a dozen darkly oily bites. Near-sexual the aftertaste, the close couch sitting after all those married years until, at the movie's end credits, Leonard said, "I shouldn't have stayed up so late," and put himself to bed without bothering to wash the truffle off his hands.

What Constance felt as she stared at the half-dozen filled sacks, laden with various shades of red and yellow and green apples, was longing. Simple, clichéd, mid-forties female longing, the kind too messy for TV and too past its prime for any primetime. She felt old among the apples, with their implicit promise of tart, firm flesh, the cyanide of their hidden pips nothing to really fear. Another year older at the fruit loop, the fall tradition of buying as much overpriced fruit as the couple could afford from the mini-farms scattered through the gorge. Agricultural tourism at its finest.

"We'll do what we always do, eat a few and throw the rest away," she answered as he hauled more bushels and pecks into their two-bed motel room. One bed for them, one to cushion both their suitcases and their fruit. She unfolded her rumpled fruit loop map to survey the orchards to hit the next day.

"My mom would've made a pie," Leonard said as he lined up the bags like children in a school photo, short to tall, fat to thin. "Probably your mom, too."

I'm married to someone winded from lugging around three bushels and four pecks, she thought. "Why did we pay for a river view if we aren't going to open the curtains?"

Leonard never answered.

A yearly vacation for a couple married over twenty years stops meaning motel sex and late-night steak dinners, complete with baked potatoes smothered in butter and cream. Leonard and Constance vacationed with thought. Who, at their age, could eat steak past seven without a night of heartburn? They agreed to the philosophy of eating for longevity after a pre-diabetic scare for him and one foot in perimenopause for her. These vacationers shunned morning donuts for muesli, after-dinner cocktails for green juice, shaken not stirred, with enough time allotted before bed to read. The Russians for him, anything translated—Spanish, German, Japanese—for her. The couple liked to vacation with a wall of dark, pondering stories between them, except when the heartburn came out of nowhere. Leonard clutched his throat.

"You scared me." Constance changed into sensible pajamas without him glancing at her body. "It looks like you're grabbing your chest."

"Do you always have to be so dramatic?"

"I'm not being dramatic. It's just that my father died so young."

"Sixty-two isn't that young," he said between burps.

"Neither is forty-six."

"Would you mind running to the store for antacids? I forgot to pack mine." Leonard settled on his side of the bed, Tolstoy in one hand, the other still gripping his throat.

Constance stared at her flannel. "Like this?"

"You should probably wear a coat."

"But I'll need to brush my hair, and my teeth, and put on lipstick. I knew we shouldn't have tried the chutney. Dipping crackers in those tiny pots is so germy, if you really stop to think."

Leonard peered over his open book. "If you knew it would be a problem, why'd you drag me to a fruit stand famous for its small-batch chutney?"

"Because I grew up on the west coast. I don't even know what chutney is."

"Apparently it's heartburn in a jar." Leonard watched her apply peach lip gloss without a mirror. "Could you also pick up more muesli, the kind with nuts? You must've forgot how at home I only eat the kind with nuts."

Constance covered her pajamas with a raincoat—required packing for the trip, along with a sewing kit, laxatives, hand cream, Epsom salts. Everything but the nightly antacids that made Leonard look like he was foaming from the mouth while lecturing to her about his newest understanding of some passage from *Anna Karenina*.

Before she shut the motel door behind her, Constance turned to ask, "Doesn't calling the two main characters by the same name confuse you?"

"The main character is named Anna, so no."

"But so are her maid and her daughter. And what about the two Alexeis?"

"Tolstoy is making a statement on adultery, I think. It's too complicated to explain with heartburn. Can I please have my antacid before the chutney kills me?"

"No one's ever died from a bout of chutney," she said as she shut the motel door, having no idea if this was true.

She'll admit to anyone who asks, but who would ever ask, that Constance moved slowly through the store, the way one kills time waiting for a pharmacist to fill a prescription. She chose generic antacids to save a dollar. When none of the other few late-night shoppers were watching, she placed the foil-wrapped roll in her coat pocket, not with the intention to steal, but to free her hands for exploring. A store where no one knew her. What a thrill to be anonymous as she squeezed five avocados for ripeness, having no use for avocados. A faint memory swam to the front of her thoughts about an elderly aunt from Minnesota who called avocados "butter pears." The memory saddened her the way any hint of nostalgia forced her to lock her brain up tight, batten down the hatches of that fine line between kitsch and melancholy where the long-dead aunt took up permanent residence. She would've hated Leonard, the aunt with the knit teapot cozies and wonderfully buttery shortbread. Constance never thought she'd end up married to a man who forbade butter in the house. And cream. And chocolate, shellfish, anything but the missionary position, most magazines, and salt.

In the bakery, Constance opened one of those cheap tubs of chocolate chip cookies with the chemical undertaste of mass production, ate one, and resealed the plastic. She never imagined herself as a grocery store night feeder, a stealer of one purloined green grape, a smeller of roses opening in black buckets near the grape and berry counter. In the beauty aisle, she tried on seven shades of nude nail polish before settling on Ballet Slipper, a shiny taupe, to carry on a passionate affair with her pocketed antacids as she walked towards the self-check.

Constance liked being alone. She paid for three spicy chicken wings from the wings and olive bar, devoured them by the closed deli area, wiped her hands on a plastic tablecloth weighted with the types of crackers assholes like

Leonard served at parties, always bland, always overpriced. What a joy, also, to leave her cell phone in the car, to feel the antacids and the polish bucking against each other the way she never had with her husband, even in youth.

An affair. Maybe that was the answer, but with whom, and where? What kind of man wants a woman with hot flashes and thinning eyebrows, no matter how many times her doctor checks her thyroid?

The next long, slow checkout line of hungry bachelors and stoned line cooks provided Constance time to exorcise the memory of butter pears from her psyche. She skimmed a magazine article about a woman who decided to have an affair with her own husband. Boring, weird, pointless, insane, names the writer's friends called her, but she swore turning her longtime partner back into her lover saved the couple from an imminent breakup.

Constance paid for the magazine and the polish. She left the antacids in her pocket, so illicit, and set off to be reprimanded at the motel for the lateness of the hour. Leaving herself enough time to digest the article before she unlocked the motel door, she found Leonard asleep, Tolstoy weighting his lap, rumors of the lethal chutney doing nothing but possibly invading his dreams.

Morning greeted her with a husband who never failed to carry grievances into a new, unspoiled day. Constance refused to play into his sour mood with her usual dose of breakfast salt, which, according to the same magazine, women hipper and younger than her, "woke" women, referred to as "shade."

"You look very handsome today," she said, and really wanted to mean it as the crunch of Leonard's muesli echoed off the wood paneling.

"You forgot to bring back my favorite kind with the mixed nuts."

"It was one of those tiny tourist stores. No nuts."

Through loud mouthfuls of cereal, bowl balanced on his lap as he leaned against the headboard, Leonard said, "The nuts are already in the cereal. You don't sprinkle fresh nuts on top, though you could."

"They were all out of the kind of cereal that comes with nuts, or raisins."

"That's preposterous."

"I swear it's the truth."

"This place is ridiculous. We spent god knows what yesterday on apples." He got up to dump his leftover cereal in the motel toilet.

"Thirty-six dollars, dear." Constance fought with the sound of that emphatic, industrial flush.

"What?" he yelled over the sounds of cleaning his bowl, rinsing his spoon, good, tidy, boring husband sounds; the sounds of a man who always returns his library books on time and knows the correct postage for any letter, has never had one stray ear hair or unaccounted dollar in his checking account. A crossword puzzle in pen with no mistakes kind of husband.

"Thirty-six dollars, dear. The Black Beauties cost the most. Why don't we try one right now, out of the sack?"

"First, they aren't washed. Second, I just ate. Third—"

But before Leonard had a chance to stop his wife, Constance stuck her Ballet Slipper painted fingernail, she had also shoplifted a lip gloss to match, into the middle of a bushel bag to fish out the darkest Black Beauty, twice the size of any grocery store variety. She set the apple in the middle of the bed, took off her pajamas and her sensible beige underwear, and waited for Leonard to come find her.

"I already apologized a dozen times. I didn't realize you were too tired to, you know—" Constance nursed a cup of coffee at a cafe up the road from the motel known for hearty egg breakfasts. She coveted the plates of bacon languishing in their grease at surrounding tables.

"Because you didn't take my chutney incident seriously."

Dropping her voice, she spoke to her lukewarm coffee, "Stop the presses. Breaking news: Chutney Incident Leads to Impotence."

"Go ahead. Mock me." Leonard cracked his knuckles, a habit when fatty food invaded his orbit.

Bacon, bacon, my kingdom for one slice of bacon.

"All I mean is I didn't know you wouldn't be able to perform."

"Jesus, keep your voice down. I can perform just fine, when I feel like performing."

"So you just don't feel like 'performing' with me?"

"It's not that." Leonard's checked watch revealed the time to him multiple times a minute. "Shouldn't we get to the last two orchards on your list?"

"I must've lost the list." Constance picked up the folded fruit loop map, cross-referenced with her bold black lettering and her tentative blue dashes. She tore the map into several pieces small enough to fill an ashtray, if they still allowed customers to light up in coffee-and-egg cafes.

"Constance, what are you doing?"

"My name isn't Constance." Constance glanced around the cafe. A stack of games to entertain customers while they waited for eggs to become omelets crowded a corner shelf near the bathroom. "It's Domino." She admired the box of white tiles, all those black dots.

The server brought the check. Leonard grabbed the green receipt from Constance. "So first you ruined our map, and now you want me to call you Domino?"

"Because that's my name."

"So you said. Show me your wallet."

After flagging down the server, Constance ordered a plate of strawberry blintzes with extra whipped cream. She stared into her small purse.

"I must've left my wallet in the room. I know it's our first date, but I hope you don't mind paying. I can make it up to you when we get back."

"By getting rid of the goddamn chutney? I saw a jar of that infernal garbage in your grocery sack this morning."

Constance had no memory of buying chutney.

"And give me your purse."

She handed over the narrow cross-body, purchased with the hope of making her own widening hips look slimmer. The contents—wallet, stolen lip gloss, a bottle of chutney the size of a mini-bar ketchup—rattled across their sticky tabletop.

"I swear I don't know how that got in there."

The chutney rolled towards Constance like the admonition of guilt. Leonard showed her the driver's license with her (bad) photo in the top left-hand corner.

"Or your wife's wallet. I'll be sure to return it with my apologies—after I'm through with you."

"Can't you just quit the drama so we can go home? If we leave now, maybe we can get back before dark?"

"Taking me home to meet the wife?" Constance shoved overly-large blintz bites into her mouth, chewed without closing her glossy lips. "Risky, but why not?"

Leonard motioned to a spot in the air parallel to her whipped cream lips. "You have some on your face."

"Where?"

"There."

"Then wipe it off. Don't be shy."

"Connie come on."

"Who?"

He dunked a corner of a paper napkin in his cold coffee, made the smear bigger in his attempt to clean his wife's face. "Sorry I guess I—"

"Just kiss it off me, then. I'm waiting."

And she was as surprised as anyone when Leonard leaned in, almost close enough to smell his breath. Close enough to see deep into his seashell-pink ear as he turned to glance at customers glancing at him, that perfectly beautiful, always wax-less ear, the ear on a statue, not the ear of a human layered with that unfortunate but accepted buildup of dust, shed skin, the very lubrication that helped him hear better, which then led to the proliferate husband ignoring the wife syndrome; what she wouldn't give to see something messy about Leonard, a ball of those yellow-orange armaments to soften those immeasurable, extra-sharp arpeggios screaming from the first chair violin in some classical piece he listened to non-stop every laundry day. She didn't know the name of the piece, what drew her husband to the movement, and more than that, why she had never asked him about music that invaded their house countless hours a day.

Clean as a whistle, fit as a fiddle, eardrum as tight as, well, a drum, her husband actually, hand to whichever god you prefer, leaned in close enough to kiss her, so she kissed back, soft and sweet, long and hard. While Leonard kept his eyes closed Constance placed a whole strawberry in his mouth. Sugar-sweetened and softened in its own juices, the strawberry glowed as if Leonard was trying to swallow a very big jewel from a very important sovereignty, before he closed his lips around the nearly neon-red orb.

Before he had a chance to bite down, Constance pressed her mouth to Leonard's, coaxing him to deposit the pristine strawberry, now warm from his mouth, into her mouth. She remembered how he had once told her about a woman whose husband got sick when she placed his used peach pit in her mouth. Or did she see that one on a sitcom, a fabled two-week peach season in a time before people looked up everything they saw, heard about, thought of online, until the looking up, that ubiquitous internet confirmation, hung over every aspect of life, even more than religion in the most religious say-a-prayer-before-eating households. Did the people who made up stories about famous peaches know about Columbia Gorge apples? Was she the apple of Leonard's eye as his warmed fruit weighted her own tongue?

FOUR VIEWS

1. A Mermaid Visits Rexall Drugs

Sometimes it's easier this way, to hide my guilt where no one really knows me, wrapped in a white paper sack stapled shut to protect my privacy.

For an hour each week, my legs come back. The first time I grew legs, days after my sailor brought me to shore, me pretending to be rescued because even a sea creature knows every man needs to pretend to rescue every woman, I marveled at their vocation. To walk. To run. To climb into hips and the secret pact women hide between their thighs; to flare into such majestic toes, ten resilient stones designed to meet the hardness of the world. Now I don't really notice: legs, toes, fins, tail, only tools to raise me out of the salty backyard pool to my favorite place on earth.

There are no pharmacies where I come from. There isn't much of anything where I come from but shells. Down there of course we wear shell bras. And too many shell bracelets and necklaces to count. We even have shell lamps with real shell shades, but nowhere to plug them in. Up here, you have drugstores with lipstick no tide will wash away. Soda fountains with so many flavors of ice cream. Wart remover, hair gel, an unending field of cotton balls.

For my sailor each week I buy a box of Old Spice, then stack the cologne like red bricks under the bathroom sink. I stay loyal to him, mostly because I hardly ever leave my pool, and he does barbecue close to the deep end, handing me my dinner on a real plate with a real napkin that doesn't stay dry for very long.

But the sole reason why for one hour a week I don't miss my dorsal fin is fish oil. Omega-3 fatty acids double-bonded at the third carbon atom. The anti-aging serum of the deep. I buy as many bottles of pills as can fit in my purse, in the highest dose possible, and the pharmacist never asks.

The first dose, two pills shining in my palm like precious jelly, I take in the parking lot before I even start my car. When no one is looking. While my legs begin to numb and I know it's time to head home. The more pills I take, the louder my heart beats, strong, steady, harmonizing with my bones as they arc into the hidden white wonder of configuration. My hair grows long, and I let it grow longer after each 500-milligram swallow, so long that sometimes all the next-door neighbor sees from his window are my blonde highlights floating out across the pool water.

But as I float, displaced from Sirenum Scopuli, smelling now of Jovan Island Gardenia Cologne and coconut Lip Smackers, I do wonder if I've just swallowed someone I used to know. That one Skipjack tuna I loved for a summer as we swam together in the pelagic zone, his rough corselet rubbing against my eager blue fins, all the promises I thought I heard him whisper through so many bubbles, all the promises I swore to almost keep.

2. *Power Couple*

It was fun at first, our game. The way, when no one was looking, I lassoed him towards my waist, a playful running bowline, the truth-telling slipknot that never let him get away.

With anything.

The pillow talk in his left ear, jokes about how my bracelets were tailor-made to match a wedding ring. Princess-cut diamonds, bezel set. That one little green stone to keep him in line, to keep him from bending me over the edge of any edge in sight when I didn't want to be bent over anything.

How the ore started out red, the way most valentines do.

The way most kisses do.

The way I've memorized his history. The way he always forgets mine, so hung up on the idea of dating a woman formed from clay that the "Man of Steel" turns clay into mud around all his friends.

Think kiddie pool. Think two-for-one margaritas. Think women wrestling to overpower each other in a way where nobody wins, Jimmy Olsen twittering a sideline play-by-play.

It was fun at first, our game. Me always on top, his wrists tied to the bedpost, no lies revealed because he never lies. But then his dirty talk about leaping tall buildings in a single bound made me think of nothing but 9/11, made me wonder how come he wasn't there.

And where was he? And where was I?

And what happened to all the silverware from that restaurant at the top of one of the Twin Towers bending in on itself, the way he likes to show-off at breakfast, serrating the edges of my teaspoons with his bare hands to separate the ruby jewels of grapefruit from the pith.

And how being faster than a speeding bullet isn't always the best thing, so I fantasize about Captain America.

His round shield. His big white star. His patriotic body so limitless in its potential, our afterglow nothing more than the star on his costume and the stars on my costume shining towards each other in the dark. Something more than shining, really. Something more than being super at one thing or wonderful at something else. Something more than stacking up our defeated villains like thin cakes. Something more than the early-morning workouts and the Muscle Milk and the Power Bars. Something more than finding the right tailor and finding the right allies and denying the breast implants and the chin implants and the hair extensions.

Something more than all of this.

3.   *The Fifty-Foot Woman Ponders the Fermi Paradox*

She knows he's out there, somewhere in the universe of so many assumed universes. A man her size made just for her.

The man her size made just for her waits on a planet her size. A planet with its own version of James Dean and its own version of Elvis and its own version of nail polish and frozen yogurt machines.

Its own version of everything she needs a magnifying glass to love now, James Dean in his red jacket pulsating his misunderstood coolness onscreen, almost too small for her big, sad eyes to see. The voice of Elvis, who she once let half-lull and half-lust her to sleep, so tinny in her cavernous ear. A Munchkin sound more than a *Love Me Tender* sound. *Are You Lonesome Tonight?* on the tiny little record smaller than her pinkie nail, careful, be careful not to break it between your ungainly fingers, nothing more than a bug munch, a termite aperitif, maybe even a high-pitched plea for help.

At the recycling center near an abandoned house she dreams she once fit in, once shaved her legs in, once made beef stroganoff for a man long forgotten, the fifty-foot woman collects pieces of paper. Confetti she tapes together until a letter emerges that can fit in her hands.

Night after night she tries to sleep propped against the eaves of the house, the empty kiddie pool from summer a makeshift blue pillow still smelling of wet grass. That squeak when she shifts her ribs away from the rain gutter.

Night after night she ponders how to write a love letter to someone she hasn't yet met. How to begin. Where to find enough ink in her search for someone her size to dress up for. Someone to know her inside, different from the man who climbed her body on a dare, anchor attached to her pubic hair, the walls of her vagina too slippery to scale, though she felt a vague desire as he lost his footing once, as he slipped his carabiner towards the overwhelming center of her pleasure.

Night after night she looks at the stars, closer to their silver crackle than any other woman on Earth. Almost close enough to reach for the man her size made just for her, obscured by clouds, by her universe, maybe by another woman in her way. She tilts her ear almost close enough to hear the first word of the first song they will dance to by a fire or by a stream or inside a cocktail bar. A new kind of drink on a new kind of table she's never heard of. Something almost like a cherry floating in her glass.

4. *Fishwife*

I guess it's just one of those things. An attraction thing. A love thing. A soul thing. Not quite a sex thing, since he can never leave his tank at the aquarium where I sit and observe him swimming around the dark, murky confines each day from ten until six. He is a rockfish. More specifically, a gopher rockfish. Mottled olive skin. Well, not exactly skin like you or I have but, since this a love thing, a soul thing, let me call it skin.

That speckled olive, red or brown in some places when the submerged lights hit, pulse, diffuse, fleck white rows like precious stones around his lissome dorsal-fin skin. Fifteen perfect inches of skin, fish, fins. A plump filet saved from its plate by the friend of a friend, hooked in tight to water conservation, her charity thing, her feeding her bored rich soul thing, so I can memorize his full orange lips with their cobalt tinge. Black eyes with an iridescent blue halo circling each round lens. He can see me this way, right through the glass. In fact, I'm pretty sure he can see through me, too. My husband would not understand any of this, but husbands, as a rule, don't understand much.

Like the one hundred and sixty dollars missing from our checking account each month that I spend, really I sacrifice, just to see him, my fish without a name after all these months. Who am I to name him? Plus, I figure if we ever meet each other beyond the glass, two almost lovers almost loving each other in a touch pool, he floating to the surface, me, the strange though familiar hand, the nails painted the color of fish scales, the thick scarred indent where a wedding ring used to be, before the touch tank, before him, I'll just let him tell me his name himself.

For now I will refer to him as him, and will until this story finds its end.

CAKEWALK

Each house the couple moved into for the two-to-three-year duration of a project came with almost identical furniture. Overstuffed ecru couches with matching love-seats in living rooms designed to show television programs to large groups of people. Entertaining houses, everyone in Ben's business designing low-cost apartments called them, though Tasha hated to entertain. Not born a "girl's girl" meant she was not a "wife's wife." She never threw dinner parties. She did not send thank-you notes.

While Ben worked long hours pushing for real tiled floors in each unit, Tasha spent her afternoons wandering the newest house like a ghost invited to a very chic, but very lonely, purgatory. If anyone on those afternoons asked what was wrong, she would answer nothing, and everything. Nothing looked wrong on the surface of her life, her couches, her clothes, but everything felt wrong under the seams. Some afternoons, while she sat on the ecru couch, a microwaved entrée balanced on one knee, she folded back the hems of her shirt, her pants. A jolt spread through Tasha every time. No hidden message waited inside a silky dart. Some simple, irrefutable fact.

You are in the wrong life, with the wrong man. This is a trap. Escape.

You are in the right life, with the right man. This is a trap. Escape.

Other afternoons, hems forgotten, she turned on the shower faucets in each of the four bathrooms to let the water run, hard and hot, for hours at a time without stepping in. Getting lost in the fog inside one's own house is never as impossible as it sounds.

Tasha met each new wife whose husband worked with Ben, almost always at an athletic club. These wives talked about the same things as all wives of rich-ish husbands. Organizing charity events, taking a cooking or conversational language class, the latest book club pick. The women, as they worked out next to each other, looked and sounded like beautifully lean parrots, Tasha thought, though she had little to discuss beyond those topics, either.

"You moved here just in time for the annual cakewalk," Chloe, newest wife since the new move, said. The first original topic Tasha had heard in years. Chloe spun her slender legs on a stationary bicycle. Her phone vibrated in the cup holder. "Sorry, I'm getting more cake updates."

Tasha huffed on the treadmill next to her. "What's a

cake update?"

"You don't have a cakewalk in your hometown?" For some reason Chloe, who had grown up here, the pretty, breathy blonde with all the dirt, let Tasha into her circle. "Every woman bakes one."

"For charity?" Tasha's breath sputtered from too much treadmill and too many takeout lunches. "Could a man bake one?"

Chloe peddled her legs like a stridulating insect. That yellow whipped cream flip of her hair.

"It's only for women. One cake and you're in. Like, *in* in. Oh, look," she said, showing Tasha a beaming pink photo on her phone. "I just got an alert about the Cherry-Blush Nut Cake. It might not be for me, though. Remember how the morning Cake Bulletin said people are shunning red food coloring now? Have you heard they get the color from crushing bugs?"

"Are you making a joke? Cake update, Cake Bulletin. Did Ben put you up to this?" Tasha's words rose over Chloe's head to catch in the blades of the gym fan recirculating the *eau de parfum* of other affluent women.

"Of course not. Look," Chloe pointed to the television hooked high into one of the club walls, "the afternoon bulletin just started."

Where the local news had flashed weather updates moments before, a shock of electric blue now filled the screen, the words "Cake Bulletin" swirled in red. A woman seated at a news desk read about the history of chiffon cake while a grainy, jumpy film of the Brown Derby restaurant ran in the background.

"Don't you think it's funny a person named Harry *Baker* invented the cake? That restaurant really did look like a big brown hat. I wonder if they had the cakewalk back then?" Chloe sipped from a water bottle. Her upper lip glistened.

Tasha wondered if she was having some sort of "spell," what her mother called words not quite making sense. "I'm not feeling well."

"You pushed yourself too hard your first day. Oh cool, an update for White Moon Cake. Who wouldn't want to try a piece of that?"

"Yes, I'm just really tired." Tasha tried not to see Chloe's phone, but turned her head too late. A photo of a three-layer white cake, frosted bright yellow and ringed in a swath of orange buttercream ribbons, came into view. Nausea churned through her as she watched the bulletin conclude on the club television with a short piece about the ongoing debate over eight-inch versus nine-inch round pans. Tasha touched her brow, surprised her skin felt so cold. "What happens if I don't enter the cakewalk?"

"If you choose not to take part, you and Ben might as well pack your things. It would be that bad."

Tasha stopped walking. An odor she did not like settled around her as she turned off the treadmill and wiped her sweat from the handles. She added her towel to Chloe's tight, folded pile in the bucket loaded with used towels, as if, towel to towel, the two women formed a less painful version of the needle-prick blood sisterhood of early teen slumber parties.

After pretending to enjoy the workout, and pledging to work out again to grill Chloe about the alternate universe her husband had stuck her in this time, Tasha agreed to download the cake update app. She then walked downtown to sign up for a library card, as she had promised her new friend. Chloe had told her that the best recipes came from the library's vintage baking book section.

A vague idea swirled somewhere in the back of her mind about why she desired to please a woman she had just met. She felt like she knew Chloe, and not just in the way she reminded Tasha of one of those good-looking girls in high school who are almost never nice.

A quote by Martha Stewart flanked the library entrance: "I think baking cookies is equal to Queen Victoria running an empire. There's no difference in how seriously you take the job, how seriously you approach your whole life." To Tasha the library looked more like a cathedral from one of those European travel shows. As she studied the dark green sculpted ivy tendrils ringing the front door, she realized the vines were lines of frosting squeezed from pastry bag frescos held with invisible hands.

Once she was inside, the head librarian directed her to

the double row of vintage baking books, displayed with a prominence saved for presidential biographies.

In response to her confused look the librarian said, "Chloe texted you might be coming. I almost missed it, though, I was so engrossed with that story about the history of chiffon cake. Did you catch it? Completely riveting."

An itch spread across her body. "Yes, I couldn't take my eyes off it."

"A group of us run the cakewalk each year as a sort of community outreach."

"Is that why the Martha Stewart quote is above the front door?"

"Why wouldn't we quote Martha Stewart?"

Spines exhaled mildew as Tasha ran her fingers over racks dominated by Betty Crocker. "I've heard Martha bakes a pretty mean cake, and at least she's a real woman. Betty Crocker is, like, completely made-up. As a librarian, I'm sure you already knew that."

"That's not the sort of rumor you want to spread around here." The librarian pushed up her sleeves, ran a hand across her forehead to straighten a crooked section of fringe.

Tasha picked up the library's copy of *Betty Crocker's New Picture Cook Book*. "This book has been around since the early sixties, but it looks brand new?" She pointed to the woman on the spine. "Don't you find it ironic that all those decades ago women struggled to emulate another woman who isn't real?"

"Ironic?"

"I studied her in a college research and analytics class. A flour milling company conceived Betty Crocker in the twenties as a marketing tool, and she became the mascot of General Mills. Over the years she's had eight portraits done, but the company hasn't commissioned a new one in almost twenty-five years. What do you think that's about?" Tasha studied a tall cake on the cover, frosted in what looked like mounds of glossy pink marshmallow. "Who could make one of these in real life?"

"It's surprising what gets turned in to the cakewalk."

"Don't you think it's a little crazy Betty Crocker cookbooks were supposed to push feminism forward? As if."

The librarian tilted her head at a slight angle. She said nothing.

"The books turned baking for your own family into something husbands could almost respect. I'm sure that was huge back then. Not like I grew up that way. We didn't have family dinner, let alone dessert. But who did?" Tasha flipped through a few more pages before shelving the book. "So you said the cakewalk is a community outreach? Like, you offer ingredients to women who can't afford them?"

"Something like that." The librarian straightened the

Betty Crocker tome. "After you make your book selections, why don't you check out our reference area, learn a little more about us?"

The librarian marched away from Tasha as if trying to appear authoritative in her beige sweater and Dansko clogs, *Betty Crocker's New Picture Cook Book* removed from the shelf again and tucked under her arm.

Small-town women weren't any different from city women. Over the years, Tasha concluded that most women, if not all, loved to organize themselves into groups, with a very determined hierarchy. Head librarian, head fundraiser, head of the committee to raise more money for Head Start, head gossip, head baker.

Tasha selected a candy-colored stack of baking books, mostly Betty Crocker. She tried to recall ever having read a cookbook as she carried her bounty to the reference area, comprised of a few tables arranged under a shadowbox display of every mayor since the town's incorporation, along with candid snapshots of the cakewalk chairs.

Ben never responded to her text about the event being *the* event of the season. As she scanned the chair head photos, dating back to the fifties, Tasha assumed the husbands were behind all of this the way husbands are always behind everything. *Elsie Pritchard, 1959 chair, did your husband run the now-defunct flour mill? If so, I'm sure you knew Betty's backstory. Char Preston, 1971, did you feign your married orgasms each night with the town sheriff? Or the mayor?*

No, that year the mayor was a woman. Tasha bent closer to the wallet-sized photos of each mayor, the state seal floating on a dark blue curtain above their heads. Female mayors all the way back to the year of the first cakewalk. Men dominated the wall before then, with their self-assured half smiles, but after 1951, women ruled the shadowbox.

Ben never mentioned the pile of baking books on the kitchen counter. Once a man becomes a husband, Tasha wondered, does his eyesight narrow its line of focus?

That night she counted the meatballs from a takeout container of spaghetti as the new house refused to settle in around her. Something about this town, and this house, disconnected her from her own autonomy, almost as if she watched the entirety of her day unfold like a member of an audience. Tasha rolled the extra, sacrificed meatball onto Ben's plate, half in apology for not working outside the home, though they didn't need the extra income, and half in apology for not doing much inside, either. She never cooked, and definitely did not bake. The meatball from the mediocre Italian place up the street with the burned garlic bread taunted her, prostrate on its rivulet of sauce, her rising yet undefinable resentment unnoticed as she aimed those feelings towards Ben and his perpetual tableside texting.

Because he can respond to every text, always, but mine. Who is he texting this late at night? Listen to the way he chews his garlic bread around its blackened edges, for the first time without protest.

"Do you notice anything about the meatballs?" Tasha almost asked the profile of her husband's face, tilted towards his phone close enough to kiss the screen, but instead said, "There's a quote by Martha Stewart engraved above the library entrance. Isn't that kind of strange?"

"Who?" He continued to text.

"The domestic diva of all domestic divas."

"Didn't she go to jail?"

"Yes, but now she's stronger and more powerful than ever, even after she dissed Gwyneth Paltrow in that famous Thanksgiving issue of her magazine featuring two pages of pie recipes called 'Conscious Coupling.'"

"I don't know what you're talking about, but I guarantee the library could have thought of a million better people to quote."

"Remember when Gwyneth called her divorce conscious uncoupling?"

"Was that before or after she got sued for putting jade eggs up her, you know."

"Way before, but not pre-Goop. I could look it up?"

"I really don't care for either of them." Ben continued to text.

"And the pie thing must've pissed Gwyneth off,

because then she ran a recipe on her site called the Jailbird Cake. It's a no-bake cake rimmed in black bars, like what Martha saw in prison."

"What's a no-bake cake?"

"I never heard of one until I watched the late-afternoon Cake Bulletin. It ran right before you came home, but I'm sure there's a nightly episode we can catch." Tasha sliced her second meatball into thinner coins. "Do you think it would be unusual if this town only had female mayors since the fifties?"

Ben paused before responding to his latest text. Bread crumbs stuck in both corners of a mouth always too dry, or too moist, to kiss.

"It would be unheard of on earth, and possibly Mars."

How rude, she thought. How condescending in a way Tasha could never explain to her husband, even if he gave her countless hours, and the fuel of his extra meatball, to try. "But it's not. I saw their photos at the library today. Every one of them women, for years and years."

"Then my guess is you were seeing wrong. And what's a Cake Bulletin?"

"I'll explain it to you sometime when you aren't busy."

"I'm not busy," he spoke to the screen.

Ben's texting usurped his meal. He let his extra meatball get cold. Tasha cleared the plates, the extra meatball still sitting, untouched, because a builder of buildings never memorizes the straightest route between the dining table and the kitchen sink.

"Seeing wrong doesn't even sound right," she said.

"I need to go to the site and work out a little kink before tomorrow's first inspection. Don't worry if I'm late." He stood from the table, patted his chest, burped into a cupped hand before leaving out the side kitchen door.

After the first years of marriage, Tasha recognized how Ben's criticism that she never cooked for him disguised itself as acid reflux. Hoping the kink he mentioned really did involve the job site, she arranged the library cookbooks in a semicircle on the living room rug. Feelings of both indulgence, at sitting cross-legged in front of so many books with a kitchen to tidy, and nostalgia tucked in around her as the late night moved towards early morning. She reminisced about a place and time she had never known, where wives baked cakes and their husbands loved them for it.

Was this once the way things worked? Her mother gone from cancer, her father just gone, she had no one left to ask as her fingertips dried from the hoary pages she thrummed between her hands, that sound of pages turning, that expanding and unexpected excitement, head down, eyes taking in the colored surge of cake illustrations between each set of directions. *Blueprints*, she thought as she read recipes for Airy Fairy Foundation Butter Loaf and Cherry Nut Angel. Lord Baltimore, Hummingbird, Spice

Berry, Pink Heaven. Names blending with the vibrant photographs reminded her of the afternoons she spent clicking her way through internet porn after her takeout lunch but before her takeout dinner. Pineapple Festival. Velvet Delight. Blood rushed to her pelvis. Spring Rhapsody. Lovelight Chiffon. All the solitary hours she hid away in Ben's study to gaze at multiple combinations of free, wet, writhing flesh. Her husband never writhed, wet or dry, before her anymore, and she was pretty sure she didn't want him to, but no real or virtual sex had ever brought as much pleasure as studying the step-by-step instructions on how to bake and frost a Daffodil Pecan Cake with triple creamed shortening.

Tasha had never even heard of single creamed shortening, let alone bought a tub of the hard, white grease. Something about Ben working out his kinks between the new building floors, maybe between the legs of some unknown woman he'd met through a secret dating app she suspected most husbands kept like little locked-up treats in the dark recesses of their phones, made her reach her hand between her own legs, right on the living room rug. Pupils dilating, heartbeat speeding, she read phrases like "add sugar and cream well" and "add hot cream to remaining sugar."

Pleasure pulsed through her, the quick, needy kind with little technique and much less finesse. A short burst that alerted her body of more to come if she would just slow down, think about all the things that bothered her, irritated her, saddened her all at once, then again, in a great giant breath, let everything go. Every single dissatisfaction, large to small, the quarts of milk Ben forgot to bring home, the ten pounds she gained and lost hundreds of times, the ecru rug too stiff beneath her pajama bottoms.

Tasha accepted her pleasure. This is a bigger feat than it sounds on paper. *I deserve pleasure. I deserve this. I deserve.*

Crawling into bed much later, body sore from too many hours sitting on the floor, Ben still nowhere close to being home, Tasha vowed to push that pleasure forward to the next day, and the next. Spurred on by a new desire to learn how to bake a magnificent showstopper of a cake to donate to whatever charity the town board saw fit, Golden Harvest, Catch-A-Valentine, Tasha hoped baking was synonymous with creating roots. A great taproot of flour and sugar and butter. Bloom where you are planted. Bake where you are blooming.

The next morning Chloe texted to ask Tasha to help set up the cakewalk. She sent several long texts full of information about how the cakewalk raffle worked, how many people to expect, tricks for having her cake picked over all the others.

"Will there only be one winner?" she texted back.

Tasha tied on an apron she had never touched, an ironic bridal shower gift folded and shoved in each new kitchen drawer in each new house under a rolling pin inherited, unused, from her mother. She flipped to the Cake Bulletin on the smaller kitchen television, midway through a discussion on whether to substitute strawberry jam for the traditional apricot between the layers of a Sachertorte. She had no pen or paper to take notes.

"Are you seeing this?" she called to ask Chloe instead of texting back and forth all morning.

"I'd say no to substituting the jam, right?"

"Exactly, though I've never eaten one."

"Me, either. So," Tasha turned off the TV, "what is the prize for winning the cakewalk?"

"Oh, it's different each year. It depends on how well you, and of course everyone else, does."

Chloe didn't laugh when Tasha said, "Sort of how the cookie crumbles? Or I guess how the cake rises. What kind are you making?"

"I'm not sure yet."

"What kinds have you made in the past?" Tasha loved sizing up the competition. She found a small yellow notebook in an already full junk drawer under the coffee pot. Apricot jam, chocolate ganache, she scribbled.

"You know, just cake."

"I get it. It's all a secret. I'll use the next few weeks to practice, and I'll be there to help you set up, of course."

"Yes, practice is the key." Chloe's voice faded a little. "The others have been telling me that for awhile now.

They say I don't try hard enough, but I am trying."

"Who's been saying that?"

Over the phone Chloe sounded close to crying. "The others."

Tasha had three weeks to learn how to bake. She took a different library cookbook to bed each night, plus a brand-new stack ordered online, while Ben texted beside her. With headphones plugged in while her husband turned from her in bed, she watched every Cake Bulletin, teaching herself not to question why a TV station devoted multiple parts of each news segment to sugar. In those weeks, Tasha also narrowed her cake choices and studied her frostings as Ben pretended to read *National Geographic* and not text back some mysterious entity every few minutes.

"Do you think the librarian was trying to mess with me last week? Or even Chloe? Like, throw me off so I have no chance of winning?" Tasha flipped through more books. Seven-minute Icing. Penuche Bundt. "And who are you always texting, anyway?"

"I'm not always texting."

"But when you are, who is it?"

Something about her husband had become even more unknowable to her in this new house. Tasha tried to memorize a recipe for boiled icing. Sugar, water, egg whites, repeat. Add cream of tartar. Cream. Creaming.

"Work."

"Work?" she questioned while she studied a section in an older book devoted to the scientific properties of cream of tartar. "It's not that I don't want you anymore," she spoke into the silence of the couple's bedroom after Ben stopped texting for the night, his magazine lying on the floor amid a pile of discarded subscription cards. A cookbook still sat open on her lap.

"It's not?" Ben pushed the side of his palm down the front of his boxers as if trying to plane a layer of fabric to reach everything waiting beneath.

"It's more like I don't want anyone. Maybe it's hormones, or adjusting to a new place. If there was a man to want, that man would still be you. I'm pretty sure, at least."

She toyed with whispering "potassium bitartrate" in a sexy voice near Ben's ear, but forgot what her sexy voice sounded like. Cook ingredients until they come to a boil. Beat with egg whites into stiff swirls or peaks. Stiff peaks or swirls?

Tasha closed the book a long time after Ben fell asleep with his phone in his palm. Who was this man beside her now, the snores and the lies, the stack of cookbooks he ignored? Holiday Snow. Lemon Fluff. *If I won the cakewalk, things would be different?*

The idea stuck in her head through a night of fitful dreaming straight through a silent breakfast. After sharing a grapefruit while they each read separate headlines off their phones, Tasha said, "I've decided I'm going to win this thing."

"There's always beginner's luck."

Ben dumped the grounds from his French press down the drain. Tasha forced herself not to complain about the coming kitchen clog.

"No, it won't be luck. It will be hard work. And careful study. My cake will be the best, this year or any other year. I can feel everything coming together, for both of us. I mean it."

And in that moment, she really did.

"Cool." Ben walked away from breakfast without giving her a goodbye kiss.

Tasha made a mental note to remember when they stopped kissing each other hello and goodbye. Was it four or five houses ago? Was she becoming what she promised not to become when she was too young to understand the danger of disappearing inside your own skin?

The trip to the grocery store up the street for baking supplies became a haze of memories rearranging them-selves in varying sequences of expectation and regret as Tasha selected flour, sugar, baking powder, walnuts for one recipe, cocoa for another. Ingredients she never bought from an aisle she never understood. A first date with Ben to a French restaurant. A honeymoon in Rome. No, wait, did that happen to a much more glamorous woman on TV?

In the grocery line she asked the clerk, "What are you bringing to the cakewalk?"

"It's not my chance again, yet. I have to wait my turn. Which is kinda bullshit since I found my grandma's recipe for Coca-Cola Cake. She could bake one in her sleep." She handed Tasha a sack too heavy with flour and sugar.

"What do you mean?"

"Texas Sheet Cake? Chocolate Church Cake? It's all the same. Cocoa, buttermilk, you pour in a can of soda right before it goes in the oven."

"I'm new here, but I thought every woman in town baked a cake for this thing?" She juggled the flour and sugar sack. "I was told, no matter how archaic and sexist this sounds, it's required."

The checker scanned a bag of chocolate chips with too much force. Dark morsels tumbled onto the conveyor belt from the split bag. Tasha tried, and failed, to gather each little blob roiling across the belt like those balls of mercury in the broken glass thermometers of childhood.

She continued, "I just assumed each husband bids on his wife's cake, and the money raised goes back to a women's non-profit. And do you have a garbage can before these melt?"

The checker accepted the melting chocolate like someone accustomed to handling sticky things. "A women's non-profit?"

"For equality awareness or female empowerment? I've lived in many places, and I've never seen a town with so many female mayors, like, ever. It's so unheard of, my husband doesn't believe it."

"I don't pay attention to those things. I thought the closest thing to a woman in power is the gay guy who runs the salon two streets over."

The line backed up behind Tasha. Hungry people, several packages of ground beef. "But I saw the shadowbox in the library? And a lady at the gym told me all about the cakewalk. Our husbands work together."

"You're going to get me in trouble if you don't go. Do you need help carrying the bags to your car?"

"Fine, fine." Tasha stacked her bags on top of each other. She forgot which sack held the eggs. "But I saw the library shadowbox. I know I'm not imagining things."

"I don't think you are. I just don't have time to pay attention until it's my turn to compete. Maybe next year I'll win the raffle and be eligible to try again?"

"If it's a raffle, how come I'm already signed up?"

"You're new. It's easier for judges to pick women without town roots. It's fairer that way. But it's the strangest thing, because I never have been able to figure out what happens to each year's winner, all the way back to when my mom first started competing. I think it has something to do with how much this town is divided."

"Divided?"

"The classic case of the haves and the have-nots. Only here it's even more extreme."

The bags hurt her arms. Tasha asked, "How extreme?"

"I think there are two different towns here, existing on different planes. Like that fourth dimension shit you hear about on the internet."

"I think I have?"

"I've always suspected it. Just call it a feeling. A few people can go between the two, but most of us stay stuck, trying to claw our way out of the poorer side, or cling to the richer side. The cakewalk has a lot to do with where everyone ends up. I even heard a rumor once that the rich women who don't make award-winning cakes get thrown back over here. For how long, no one knows."

"This all sounds crazy, existing in different dimensions. It sounds like science fiction."

"It does, and I don't go in for that sort of stuff. But since when does a town this size have two libraries, two down-towns, two mayors, with most everyone I ask not seeming to understand how I can see both? Think about it."

The checker scanned the next order. Tasha waited at the end of the conveyor belt, as if she had forgotten how to find her way to the parking lot.

The heat hit her when she exited the market. Spring felt different in this town. Along with the usual renewal and promise of warmth to come, this early balm brought not only flowers, but a gummy perspiration she could not tell whether she was walking through or creating from within.

Tasha left the groceries in her backseat without worry about the chocolate melting or the eggs doing whatever eggs do when they get too hot. She drove to the library and parked in a smaller lot around the corner from the lot she noticed on her first trip. Same Martha Stewart quotes flanking the front door. Inside she saw the same librarian and the same vintage baking aisle and the same shadowbox filled with the same women's faces. She flipped through a baking book from 1952. The colored pages soothed her confusion. Sugar Maple, Morocco Choco.

"Why are you letting a grocery clerk get to you? Someone so common, so ordinary. Someone so, well, beneath you." Tasha spoke towards the book.

Beneath me? Is she, or anyone else, Tasha thought as the recipes blurred in her hands, *beneath me?*

She couldn't remember the superiority spreading through her body until moving to the new town. Tasha knew, from her association with Chloe, that she had landed this time on the right side of things. It was easy to buy into her own hype. Those after-workout country club Cobb salad lunches with her new friend added to the problem, toasted with too much buttery chardonnay. Not caramel or butterscotch or peach cobbler-noted supermarket wine, but bottles straight from the Marcassin Vineyard. Diacetyl. New oak barrels. The proper glass with the

"U" shaped bowl.

On her way to the car, with no library books tucked under her arm, Tasha studied a large, faded brick building next to the lot where she had parked, Public Library stamped in white brick over the pinkish blocks. A town with two public libraries made no sense. As Tasha placed her hand on the front door of the pink building, a woman standing outside told her the library was closed.

"But I can see people in there?" She craned her neck. "And who are you, the library police?"

She pushed past the woman. Inside, a stagnant current of air settled across her face and neck. No air conditioning on such a hot day? And no bank of high-speed computers or large reference area with a focus on female poets from around the world, features she only dimly noticed in the other library. Over one desk, on which sat one dictionary, a photo collage of the town mayors since its incorporation hung behind smeared glass. All men.

"But what about the women?" she asked a librarian at a desk near the dictionary.

He looked up from a book almost as thin as a magazine with a torn cover and smudged spine. "What women?"

"All the female mayors? And all the photos of the cakewalk?"

"Oh, yes." He turned pages too quick to be reading. "You're in the wrong library. Your library is next door. I would tell you to have a good day, but your type usually does. And you'll need to leave now. You get only one free trespass before the bad thing happens."

"What bad thing?"

"Trust me, the bad thing is so bad, you don't want to know."

Back on the sidewalk Tasha stared at both buildings, believing the bad thing really would be bad, and really would happen. She vowed to avoid it the best she could. The pink library, with no rose bushes out front, no apple trees edging the sides, stood next to her library, a structure that looked like something out of *Architectural Digest*. Tasha had become so accustomed to living with self-cleaning bidets and in-floor heating, reality had moved on around her, if reality was the correct word. Or shadow. Compete. Lemon Gold Crumb. Sunburst Chiffon.

Her chocolate chips melted in the backseat without her knowing, the same way so many other things fell apart when she wasn't looking. It's not like being the wife of a builder of buildings meant anything more than not having to work, and affording to buy anything her heart desired with a click of an online button, one swipe of a credit card. She forgot about the dozen eggs, now sun spoiled, and the flour ripening its hidden weevils in the rising temperature. Privilege. The word spread through her the way a fever used to overtake her when her mom was in the final stages of dying, Tasha timing her illness with her mother's to create some sort of heritage revolving around blankets and pills instead of hand-me-down recipes.

Chloe lived close to the library. By the park, she had mentioned to both Tasha and Ben over sushi one night. Tasha almost forgot how many couple dates she and Ben went on with Chloe and her husband over the last few weeks, the women only mentioning the cakewalk if they ended up checking their lipstick together in the restaurant bathroom. After several sushi, Thai, and steak and potato dates, Tasha still forgot the name of Chloe's husband. This wasn't like her. At least she thought this wasn't like her. So foggy in the afternoon heat, two worlds bumping against each other, or she was losing her mind? How could one town sustain two libraries? Why couldn't the grocery clerk compete in the cakewalk? What the hell was the husband's name?

Closer to the park, Tasha scanned for the house she imagined Chloe spent her time juicing and reading Elizabeth Gilbert in, moving her husband's paycheck between their checking and savings accounts for that upcoming trip to the newest trendy Asian country. No houses on the block looked like her mind's image of Chloe's home. Too small. No red door. No Vitamix box broken down and stacked in the blue recycling bin near the front porch.

A blonde woman ran by in shiny pink yoga pants.

"Chloe?"

The woman stopped but kept running in place, did not turn around.

"Thank God you jogged by. I need to talk to you. It's an emergency."

Out of breath, Chloe managed, "I can't right now," before jogging on, forcing Tasha to follow.

She grabbed at Chloe's matching pink shoulder but could not keep pace enough to get a solid grip on the slippery fabric.

"Please don't make me run in these shoes. Just a quick coffee at your house. It doesn't even need to be coffee."

Chloe stopped running in front of a small house where dandelions spread their fluffy parachutes over a brown yard. "If you insist, but only because it's you." She scampered towards the gate of a fence in need of paint the way women in shape always move, as if something exciting is about to happen. Tasha followed the taut pink vision down a crumbling sidewalk and up two crumbling steps into a small house that smelled of cats.

"Where are we? Who lives here?"

"I do." Chloe sat at a card table covered with a vinyl cloth and pushed into the corner of a dining room next to a slim yellow kitchen. A tabby rubbed against her toned pink calves. "This is me."

"But I don't understand."

A feeling came over Tasha, one she could only describe

as a total recognition of this house. Not a type of house, but this specific house. She knew it, deep in the corner of her memories.

Chloe pulled a fake daisy out of a vase of artificial flowers. A few tugs at the stiff fabric petals yielded no one loving her, or loving her not. "You thought just because our husbands work together we can afford to live the way you live?"

"I did." As she sat at the card table Tasha pondered her multiple-floored house, her butler's pantry, the outdoor grilling deck. "Or I assumed you lived close to the way we do."

Tasha noticed an amalgam of smells. Mildew, dust, old pipes, too many pets. Her view, sitting at the table across from Chloe with no idea how to fold her arms, whether to cross her legs at the knees or the ankles, landed in the kitchen on a box of Pop-Tarts sitting next to a box of Fruit Roll-Ups.

"And you never told me you have kids."

"I haven't told you a lot of things."

The odors of young children, grape juice, Cheerios, piss, mixed with the rest of the odors. Tasha pulled at the arms of her sweater. Something about the smell, too familiar, too comfortable, made her even more uncomfortable. So uncomfortable, in the motionless afternoon air, an urge to cover up overwhelmed her. She looked towards the couch in search of a blanket, daring herself to pick one up without asking. Picture books crowded one end of a small sectional. It was only a couch, and would ever only be a couch, never a divan or a settee or a davenport, not the antique chesterfield Chloe had described being "madly in love with" during a workout a few days before. A blanket printed with cartoon characters heaped on the floor next to the couch. With an aversion to the pilled fleece, Tasha still longed to finger the vivid, bumpy print.

"And where's your husband? Keith? Rob? I think the shock is confusing me."

Something about this new town was getting to Tasha. Keith? Rob? James? Cinnamon Apple Cream Cake. Springtime Fancy.

And had Chloe even done her research? Did she memorize *The Checklist for a Championship Cake* from one of the very well-loved library books Tasha would turn in late, and accept the fee, so no other bakers in town could read up on secret pointers, Cake Bulletin or not? From what Tasha gleaned over the past days, a prizewinning cake was all about crumb. Color of crumb, texture of crumb, tenderness of crumb, "velvety touch from finger to tongue."

Chloe said, "At the dinner with the dragon sushi roll, it was Keith. I brought Rob to the one where you and Ben split a spicy tuna."

"Yes, Keith."

"Then Rob after that, and I can't remember who followed."

Crumbs of all colors floated through Tasha's mind.

"Are you even listening to me?"

Tasha answered after a few beats, "I'm listening, but nothing you're saying makes any sense."

Tasha tugged on the same grubby fabric flower. Her fingers yearned to touch down on something real, even if real meant rusting wire and polyester.

"People like you can never see past your ginger and wasabi to notice, so I just call someone who looks close enough to the someone before him, and for a free meal they make small talk, and sometimes even almost seem to like me."

"Keith with the dragon roll I wouldn't call on again. He didn't seem to like you at all."

"That's not the point." Chloe arranged the bendable flowers in tense, juddering movements. The petals jolted back to their original shapes as soon as she let go of each contrary stem.

"Wait, do you mean Ben doesn't work with Keith, or Rob?"

"He may, he may not. All I'm saying is they aren't my husbands. We're all just trying to hold on until the next cakewalk. If we make it one more week, everything might change."

The urge to swear at Chloe until she made sense

overtook Tasha. She wanted to get out of the house, the horrible, average, common, undersized house like the house of her childhood, and Ben's childhood. A house where nothing good ever happened. Tasha wanted to go back to her impersonal ecru house that held no memories yet, good or bad. She also kind of wanted a Pop-Tart because they reminded her of the past. She toyed with asking Chloe to warm a pastry in the ancient toaster oven with a crumb catch tray she bet no one had emptied in years.

"I once lived in a house just like yours," Chloe said. "My husband, my real husband, owned one of the largest construction companies in town."

"He sounds a lot like Ben."

"We threw catered parties. We had a butler's pantry." She walked to the kitchen faucet to fill an empty Voss water bottle from the tap. "And an outdoor grilling deck. But I always insisted I make my tapenade from scratch. Nonpareils capers, never gruesas."

"I've never understood capers, but Ben taught me how to make tapenade last summer. At least, I think it was last summer. I'm a little foggy today."

"My husband and I raised money for every charity you could name. Ben and I ruled this town. But then came last year's cakewalk."

"Your husband's name is Ben, too? Where is he now?"

"It's very hard to explain."

Tasha said, "I haven't always lived the way I do now. Growing up, I didn't have much of anything. And there was a time, before *my* Ben, I had even less. What's so important about holding on until the next cakewalk? Did something bad happen at the last one?"

"The worst thing you could ever imagine. I almost won. At least the organizers banished me to this house and not worse."

Tasha wondered how things could be worse.

Up from the table and back down in the motion of a trained athlete, Chloe grabbed a thick binder off a shelf near the card table. Yellowing recipes in a specific, antiquated cursive scattered around the vase of fake flowers. "So, I paid a dealer the rest of my life savings for these."

"Old recipes?" Tasha fingered a tattered recipe before Chloe ripped one edge as she yanked the card from her hand.

"I'm the only one allowed to look, at least until the cakewalk is over."

"Jesus, I understand it's some kind of competition, but you don't need to be so aggressive. Don't worry, I haven't decided what to bake."

"These are cake recipes from all over the country, dating back to at least the forties. The dealer couldn't prove their provenance but swore to me, which I trust because he's a friend of a friend's almost second ex-husband, that some of these are even the winners of past cakewalks."

"Here in town? Won't they recognize the cake if you turn it in again?" Tasha strained to decipher that one stained measurement for baking powder on the Pineapple Festival Cake card. Was it an alternate version of the standard three and a half level teaspoons? Could that make all the difference?

"They swore some of these cards are past winners from cakewalks all over the country, and Canada, too."

Tasha tried to glance at more of the aged cards. "If this is something that's been going on for a long time everywhere, why haven't I heard about them until now?"

Chloe pulled another card from Tasha's overly-curious, wandering fingers.

"You just can't remember the cakewalks from your past. Not can't, I mean don't. You just don't remember."

Chloe shifted the rest of the cards out of Tasha's reach before turning her back to plug in the toaster. Just enough time for Tasha to tuck a random recipe card into her jeans pocket. Three quick steps, Chloe in her kitchen. Stack, move, prance over to the outdated appliance. Did this mean Pop-Tarts were sure to follow?

"Well, which is it?" Tension pushed along her collarbone until Tasha's body felt broken in parts, then set back in an unwieldy, permanent cast. The recipe card burned through her pocket to sear her thigh. "There's a huge difference between me forgetting something or choosing not to remember."

"I don't see the difference. Do you want a Pop-Tart?"

The aroma of artificial flavors filled the small space. Chloe sliced the warm toaster pastry in half with a long, serrated knife. She halved the halves, then kept cutting the pastry until a pile of thumbnail-sized bites leaked their red insides onto a paper plate. A little frosted cherry square dissolved on Tasha's tongue like a communion wafer.

"There's a major difference. Are the town's female mayors connected to the cakewalk?" Tasha's legs wobbled a little as she stood. The familiar suction of her palms pressing and releasing from the vinyl tablecloth reminded her again of childhood.

A recipe for penuche frosting mesmerized Tasha from the top of the card stack. She would give almost anything to touch another card, divine the mystical measurements. Another teaspoon of brown sugar, or a slight temperature shift? Something told her that winning this cakewalk would be the most important thing to ever happen.

"I'm going to show you something now. But you have to promise to never tell a soul, especially not Gentle Ben."

"How'd you know I sometimes call him that?"

"Lucky guess." Chloe opened her front door. "Come on."

The two women walked down the steps towards the graying fence.

Chloe said, "Now I'm going to tell you something that sounds crazy. The only way it will make sense is if I show you."

Nostalgia rushed through Tasha as she turned to look back at the house, the nondescript, tiny thing she recognized but also wanted to forget. She already missed that which repelled and even sickened her. A cartoon blanket, artificial flowers, artificial flavors, a deficit of space.

The luxury of her space was many times not a luxury. She never paid attention to which room Ben spent his scant hours in after work. If Tasha wandered too far from the kitchen, she never could tell if dinner was burning, so decided not to cook at all. Chloe's kitchen looked just the right size to bake a whole chicken. She would know just when the skin crisped without over-crisping, even if she ran a bath after stuffing the bird with thyme and whole lemons. The creaking boards beneath her, the hidden castes of termite soldiers making their own meal of a wallpapered beam, there was safety in the comfort of baking chicken, the complexity of bugs digesting wood.

"Can you just imagine the cakes someone once made in your kitchen? Cakes we'll never get to experience in our lifetime," Tasha said. "So much history in there. Not like the soulless, already furnished places Ben keeps moving us to."

Buttercup. Lucky Clover. Chocolate Indian.

Chloe strode ahead of Tasha, in control of the spatial

difference between the two women and the world around them. A grasp towards Tasha's hand brought her up short.

"I'm not joking around. Focus."

"I already know what you're going to show me. I've been turning it over in my head all afternoon. I don't understand how it's possible, but there are two worlds here, aren't there?"

"Yes!" Chloe's body seemed to float a few feet above Tasha. She turned back. "I swear I've been losing my mind this entire year. I thought I was the only one who could see it. Our library. The other library with no poetry books written by female authors, not even Sylvia Plath. The grocery store on the other side of wherever town splits in two that only sells one kind of tampon. The male mayors, councilmen, businessmen. Too many husbands walking around in charge of everything." Chloe paused for a moment to breathe. "I'm sorry I'm not making as much sense as I hoped. I'm just shocked you can see it, too."

Chloe and Tasha stood in the center of the street. Tasha wondered if they looked like two women in the middle of a good gossip or two soldiers in a hushed strategy session before a coming battle.

"More people see it than just us." Tasha reached for Chloe's hand. "I'm positive a grocery clerk knows. She acted like a total bitch when I asked about the cakewalk. Then she threw all my things into one sack."

"I'm sure it's because she's an in-between."

"Like the guy in the other library who asked me about being in the wrong building?"

Chloe pushed back a strand of hair. A long blonde streak coiled from the perpetual rearranging to land again in the middle of her face. Her sad, panicked beauty struck Tasha.

"Oh no, the men on both sides know. Every man in this town, and every other town, everywhere, knows. They just let all of us sort it out."

"Then what's an in-between?"

"Someone like me, and the grocery clerk, and remember the librarian who showed you around the cookbook section? They all came close to winning past cakewalks. Then the organizers relocated them to the other side of town."

"I don't understand."

"And it's too dangerous for me to explain it all to you. Let's just say we saw a little too much of what goes on behind the scenes. But the thing is, the longer we all go without winning, the easier we get stuck over here. We end up forgetting. But winning has its own set of problems."

"Is it not good to win?"

"The details fuzz around the edges the further away I get from each cakewalk."

"But how could you forget the difference between living somewhere run by men and living somewhere run by women? That's like forgetting the difference between having a voice and not knowing how to speak."

Chloe leaned in so close to Tasha's face, Tasha smelled her salty, fruity breath. "It's the women who end up in the big houses with the rich husbands who end up forgetting. Women, obviously, like you. You've forgotten, haven't you?"

Tasha backed away from her. Where were all the cars, the kids out playing after school, the other women? Even Chloe's cat disappeared. Silence on a suburban street frightened her more than if the two women stood in the middle of a dark country road on a moonless night.

"Forgotten what?"

"That until a year ago, you lived here. This is your house, on this street."

Tasha thought she might faint. Her throat dried. She could not swallow. "My house? I've been married to Ben for years, and I just moved here a few months ago."

"They want you to think that, but it's not true. Because I failed at the cakewalk, and you almost won, your reward was to take my place. My punishment was to take yours."

"But I don't remember any of that."

"Who do you think Ben is texting every night? Why do you think he never touches you? He's not your husband. He's mine. And I have every intention of getting him back."

"But how is this all decided by cake baking? This is the

most backwards, archaic, insane thing I've ever heard, even if only a tiny part of what you're saying is true."

Chloe moved her tight pink body closer to the sidewalk so Tasha would follow. Chloe's sweet sweat permeated the air. Tasha moved close enough to Chloe's front yard to rest one hand on the aged gate, on possibly her old, graying gate. Did she have children, too, or was that all part of her punishment, the uncertainty?

"So, what's the solution to all of this?"

"Win the cakewalk and switch places with me. That's the only thing remotely fair. I've suffered living here long enough."

"But what about Ben?"

"What about him? He doesn't even act like you're alive."

"If everything you say is true, or even if one of us, or the other, or both, is crazy, did you approach me at the gym that first day to take away my life? Is that why you showed me which books to read and which recipes to study?"

"I'm taking back my life. This has nothing to do with you."

"I think I could win, but I think you're very wrong about what will happen to me afterwards. I think you'll be even further banished than you already are. I've been studying for weeks. I have the ingredients in my car right now to make a Lime Angel and a Chocolate Irish."

"I told you about the cakewalk not to trap you, but because those are the rules. One more loss for me and I move on to the forgetting side. If you see me in the grocery store after the cakewalk, no matter how loud you call my name and how hard you wave, I won't see you. I may be shopping, I may be a checker, but I won't remember anything about my past."

"Which will only benefit me."

"Until the next new woman moves to town and this whole thing begins again."

"The Cake Bulletin mentioned none of this?"

"Why don't you go home and ask Gentle Ben how it all works, if you don't believe me. I've already told you way too much." Chloe shut her gate behind her.

Tasha did not follow.

In the library parking lot she dug through a new pile of checked-out cookbooks. A handwritten recipe card fell from one. The words on the card first made sense before blending into undefinable swirls. Tasha felt dizzy, unlike herself, almost like she stood a few inches apart from her body but took her soul with her. She blamed the heat, the stress, as she peered in the backseat to find all of her baking ingredients just as she left them. The chocolate stayed in the shape of chips. The eggs were cool as she turned one over in her palms a few times, ran the smooth shape across her damp temples before returning the egg to the carton.

Darkness fell over the kitchen an hour earlier than Tasha expected. Her clothes stiffened as an unfamiliar perfume mixed with the aroma of chocolate cake. She remembered to add sour cream to ensure a moist crumb. As the cake raised, she studied the recipe card she found in that library book. Tasha understood the meaning, the ingredients, the potential outcome before hiding the card in a kitchen drawer her husband never opened.

A mess greeted Ben when he got home from work. Pans and bowls and beaters covered in dark, leftover batter piled in the sink. Cakes cooling in their pans took up every counter space. Tasha decided winning the cakewalk, her practice uniform complete with a dirty apron, took up more time, more room, and even more thought than she had prepared for.

"I'm onto them, and all of this, now." Tasha motioned towards the chocolate-stained suds rimming the kitchen sink. "Chloe told me everything."

"Everything?"

After struggling for a clean spot Ben set a stack of new blueprints on the kitchen counter. Not even settled into the house a year and he'd be breaking ground on a new building site in less than another.

"I know I don't belong here with you. I'm not sure how long I've known. Maybe there were brief glimmers here and there along the way, memories I can't remember, others that seem like they belong to another woman."

A diamond tennis bracelet slid down her thin wrist to knock against a mixing bowl in time to the hard stirring of another, lighter-colored batter.

"Where did you get that bracelet?" Ben pointed to the circle of square-cut diamonds hooked almost like teeth around his wife's wrist.

"I found it on the dresser this morning. Didn't you give it to Chloe for your anniversary?" Tasha stirred with her back turned to Ben until the thick batter turned pale yellow.

"No, I didn't." Ben grabbed at the bracelet.

A quick bite of pain as his fingers pressed the chilly edge of diamonds into her skin.

"And where did you get these?" He pulled at a short strand of pearls warming like tiny balls of butter around her neck. A knot between each pearl showed provenance.

"I found this in a box behind another one in the closet. They don't belong to me. It doesn't even matter anymore whether it's Chloe."

Cake after layer of cake cooled on the counter between the couple. Tasha had no recollection of how each cake came to rest on the counter, her afternoon memory as murky as trying to see herself in the bathroom mirror after a shower. The secret heirloom recipe discovered in the library book and waiting in the drawer invigorated her as Tasha tucked herself into the corner of her L-shaped kitchen.

"And why are you dressed like a 1950s housewife? Is this some kind of joke?"

She pulled a red velvet cake from the oven. "What's wrong with the way I dress?"

"You look crazy, that's what's wrong. Chloe never dressed that way. You didn't find those clothes in her old closet."

"Does a husband ever know his wife like he thinks he does?"

"How the hell did a red cake get in there? I swore you were just mixing up a yellow one a minute ago?"

"Just like I don't belong to you, maybe you don't belong to me, either?"

Ben pounced towards Tasha, but could not wrestle the hot cake pan from her oven mitts. He grabbed a handful of her gingham-check house dress. She never wore dresses, let alone a tight shirtwaist cut across her breasts with yards of fabric flowing towards her knees. Beneath her apron sat two patch pockets trimmed in white rickrack.

"I'm serious. Look at yourself. Even if we haven't known each other as long as I've been pretending we do, this is not you."

Her reflection in the microwave above the oven revealed a woman from another time, almost from another dimension. Though she had no memory of where she got the dress, whether she'd stayed up late sewing the garment as an inside joke for the cakewalk, planning to show up dressed the part of the subservient cake-baking housewife, Tasha liked the cut. The bodice elongated her waist while accentuating her breasts. The skirt folded around her legs like layers of whipped frosting. And her hair, worn straight and long, now curled close to one side of her face before waving into a loose bang above her eyes. What shocked Tasha the most wasn't wearing the hair of another woman, or ringing her neck in real pearls, the heft, the sheen, the warmth, but her pale face accented in a mouth of red lipstick, as if she had walked around for hours sucking on a piece of fruit too exotic to name.

And maybe she had? It was the strangest thing, not remembering how she'd spent the rest of the afternoon after leaving Chloe's house to retrieve her car in the library parking lot. As much as Tasha, over the past months, didn't recognize her husband, or at least any qualities that drew her to him when they first met, when she thought they first met, she recognized her own face even less. Instead of fear, though, she felt hope.

"Isn't this how you want me to be?" The bounce of her curls mesmerized Tasha's own hand with each manicured pat. She blew on the red velvet layer, hoping to cool the cake quicker. "There's no fancy name for this one," she spoke towards Ben, who had forgotten his blueprints to stare at the woman who was his wife, but not his wife. "Just red velvet. A classic cake doesn't need to be too kitschy or too cute."

"I don't like you this way. You look like you're dressed up for Halloween."

"You're silly." Tasha handed Ben the oven mitts by offering her hands to his. He removed the puffy gloves. "Can you help me take out the last one?" When she bent to open the oven door her husband bent with her, leaned towards the warm cake. As a couple, they removed the final practice bake of the evening with unexpected care.

"How silly do you think I am?" he asked close to her pearled ear.

She had him.

"But what about your wife, your real wife?"

"Chloe and I had issues. And I'll admit, I never gave you a chance. Before last year's cakewalk, you were just some woman who worked in the nearest grocery store I'd flirt with a little once a week."

"I was?"

"You were. But, if I'm honest with myself, I looked forward to those few minutes a week more than I realized. And I'm sorry I didn't make your transition here better, easier. Do you think it's too late for me to try?"

Tasha dropped to the floor in front of the oven in a gingham swoon. Her knees ached against the kitchen tile, sticky, in need of a good mopping, but she stayed in the position as she undid her husband's belt. Buckle, leather, Tasha could not remember the last time she undid his belt, or if she had ever undone his belt. The fragrance of cooling cake sweetened the room with the remembrance of her kiddie birthday parties before the other guests arrived, her mother, before illness hung around the house like scenery in a never-ending play, removing each layer with an emphatic tap on the cake pan until the cake released itself onto the waiting sheets of waxed paper.

Ben said nothing as she unzipped his pants. She tried to take him into her mouth before he knocked away her eager hands. In a move as choreographed as it was clumsy, he pinned her against the warm stove, back to him, voluminous skirt and matching petticoat billowing around her waist, pearl necklace tugged on almost too hard as he took her with little refinement, but without the self-consciousness that sometimes grows between couples—each spouse so used to seeing the same body year after year that a perverted sort of shyness takes over.

Her body was new to him and his body was new to her in the few moments before he broke free of her fabric and her flesh.

"Don't do the cakewalk," Ben said as Tasha straightened both her dress and her pearls. "Don't do the cakewalk. You don't need it anymore. *We* don't need it anymore." He fumbled for her hands. "I'm serious. Please, don't do it. We could try to make this work. Why can't we at least try?"

"Are you being serious?"

"Tash, you need to listen to me. Please don't do the

cakewalk."

She flipped a cooled cake layer onto a serving platter as if the last few minutes were already a distant memory. "How well do you know Chloe?"

"What do you mean?"

"Where was she born? Where does she live?"

"I've never believed that biography creates closeness. What we could have if we just tried?"

Ben missed a belt loop on his pants. It took Tasha several moments to decide whether or not to tell him. She decided not to tell him.

"This afternoon when I got home, I found not only Chloe's pearls, but a blonde hair wrapped around them."

"It was an obligatory present for a milestone I can't even remember anymore."

"A long, light blonde hair that coiled like an old telephone cord when I dragged the hair between my thumb and fingernails. Have you heard of that trick?" Tasha slathered thick, white frosting over one of the red velvet layers. "To tell if a girl is boy crazy? Will her little blonde hair curl under pressure? Does her skin turn yellow if you rub a dandelion under her chin?"

"I thought that was to see if you'll be rich?"

"You know about the tricks?"

"Tricks?"

"Like me finding her hidden strand of pearls? So far back in the closet, I don't think most people would've found them unless something inside told them to look. Just like when I reached my hand back even further and found a little photo of you and Chloe. A wedding photo, I think. I'm almost positive, unless you two were just playing dress-up? And that photo, those pearls, make everything else make sense?"

"How?"

"No matter how much I pretend, or whether or not I do the cakewalk, you are not mine."

"Those are her pearls. And yes, she was my wife, once, what now seems like lifetimes ago. The rest of it you haven't figured out all the way, and I'm sorry, Tash, but it's against the rules to tell you. And you're looking a little pale. You better sit down. Enough baking for today."

"You're sweet, but I'm honestly feeling better than I have in my entire life."

"Then no cakewalk?" Ben spoke towards the back of the curled head Tasha would not stop rearranging into loose finger waves with one hand as she finished frosting her red velvet with the other.

"No cakewalk," she lied. "I promise not to turn in a cake, but I can't turn my back on Chloe and not at least help her set up."

"You can't trust her. I hope, for us, that you stay far away from her."

Tasha carried a cake tray heavy with a frosted confection out of the kitchen towards the living room.

The night of the cakewalk, Tasha wore another vintage dress she found hanging in the back of her closet, but no pearls so as not to offend any judges who might be on Chloe's side. Hair up and little make-up, just one red kiss in the center of her face, she drove herself to the cakewalk with her backseat loaded. For once she did not care how late Ben worked.

The entry for her first cakewalk sat like a fantastical beacon in the back seat. White. Exquisite. The Princess of the Snow cake. The recipe card cake. The winner. The solution to either make Ben her husband, or leave, the decision finally up to her without coercion or complaint.

Four ice-white layers stood tall on a crystal cake stand between more thick, sticky drifts of marshmallow fluff. White on white on white, vanilla buttercream, silvery meringue kisses. On top of the cake, white fondant, rolled and shaped by Tasha's now deft hands, formed a small mirror image of her carrying a cupcake-sized Princess of the Snow cake, which held an even smaller figure of her holding an even smaller cake. Under a magnifying glass one could see these sugar paste ladies and their diminutive cakes go on and on until the last lady holding the last cake could fit inside a single grain of rice. The spectacle was almost too unreal to comprehend.

In the community center parking lot Tasha watched women and their husbands carrying cakes up the front steps. Chloe carried what looked like a chocolate cake frosted in more dark chocolate and studded with candy bars. Other women she'd watched working out at the athletic club or ordering sushi at the next table over on date nights steadied their cakes on plates and platters and even ornate footed stands. With so many cakes in such a long line, and with so many men in line behind them, Tasha realized her cake would only be one in a sea of competition for that unknown, ultimate prize.

Inside the large, stuffy building, decorated in streamers and smelling of industrial pots of coffee, some women adjusted their offerings on large card tables while others patted tears from the edges of their made-up eyes. Whoever had decided the stakes of the night, everyone taking part in the event corroborated its importance with their collective solemnity. Everyone except Tasha.

Ben, off work early and ready to support her, she believed, she hoped, she dared to hope, waved to her from across the hall as if he was excited to see her, cake or no cake. Chloe waved too, akin to the way Ben moved, their motions mirroring each other's. Nothing in Tasha cared, though, whether or not she was losing her husband to another woman, or had already stolen him without remembering. She did not want to win. Tasha did not want to be a part of this. What was it worth, in the end?

She made plans, quick and reckless, to take the car and run away from the new town to another new town. Or run back to her old hometown, if she could remember her old hometown, and start over again. A new life where she could be herself. Bake or not bake, walk around the park one afternoon, work at a grocery store without having to answer to anyone. Did she have a child somewhere? Had some little voice somewhere in the world called her Mom?

Tasha smiled at everyone who watched her walk towards her last name on one of the card tables.

Standing in front of her name, her perfect dress, her pleasant red mouth, Tasha picked up her cake and dropped it on the ground. Her littlest of the decorated women suffocated under the weight of so much sugar. Whiteness, but no silence, filled the space around her. All she had to do was turn and walk to her car and she'd be free.

"Congratulations, Tash," Ben, now at her side, whispered in her ear, "you won."

"But how?"

"You realized winning means nothing at all. And none of us will ever forget your sacrifice." He motioned to Chloe. She joined him as the crowd surrounded Tasha.

They filled their mouths with chunks of the dropped cake. Dozens of unknown hands covered in marshmallow pulled at Tasha's dress and tugged at her hair. In moments, something sharp shredded the fabric around her chest. Soon cold air hit her exposed back, her neck. Her skirt ripped as multiple hands yanked off her underclothes. The hair between her legs grew moist, sticky from other hands pushing bits of her own cake up inside her until no more would fit. But she refused to scream. They kept pushing until something broke, wetness, the smell of her own blood. More hands cut off strands of her hair, nipped her chin, gouged out one eye. Tasha lost her ears to scissors in two large swipes.

When the crowd picked Tasha up she was no longer herself, and no longer a woman, not really, most of her slashed, prodded, chewed in half, spit out by someone, maybe Chloe, maybe Ben, then swallowed by another. A sacrifice, they said. Thank you for your sacrifice, they said.

Right before she lost consciousness something inside her smiled. At the way things had always been. At the way things would always be.

THE KEEPER OF THE
WALDEINSAMKEIT

He likes to feed her with a sterling fork because she belongs to someone else. This is how he marks her. Sometimes he bites her, too. She imagines her blood blooming across his tongue. She imagines the smell of lavender and face powder, knowing these things do not really hide inside her. When he feeds her, he insists on using real silver. He only owns one flatware set and an old Victrola. She imagines taking the Victrola on picnics. She makes the mistake of calling it a record player. (Around him she always says the wrong things.) She tells him the voices on the other side of the needle sound too far away to be anything but dead.

"Listen to those sad sounds. We should give them all a funeral."

He feeds her a strawberry éclair, one pink mouthful at a time. He makes sure the strawberries are real, even in winter.

She read once about a woman who spent all the money

she earned to eat strawberries in winter. A true story, before everyone called true stories either memoir or autobiography. The woman called it "my story" and that was enough. She wishes people would stop demanding proof from each other now, "likes" on Facebook, Instagram hearts, a crying saint burning her image into a piece of toast.

The original Virgin Mary toast sold for $28,000. The online casino that purchased the toasted cheese sandwich vowed to donate the profits from displaying the toast to charity. This happened before the low-carb craze. The original owner swore that in the ten years she claimed possession of the sandwich, the toast shed no crumbs. The owner recalled how, a decade before, the Blessed Virgin had stared back at her as she bit into her lunch. The woman screamed for her husband. News reports did not mention if the couple were Catholic. News reports did not mention how the image on the burned bread looked more like Isadora Duncan than how everyone thinks the Virgin Mary looks.

She keeps a picture of Isadora Duncan by her bed. This has nothing to do with the Virgin Mary toast. Her Catholic friends say the dancer looks like the Virgin Mary. Her husband accuses her of morbidity when she aims her nightly prayers towards a woman killed by fashion.

"How can you canonize a woman whose head was almost pulled off by her own scarf?"

She wants to tell her husband about Isadora's last night. How she left a party in Paris with a young stranger, a French mechanic who wanted nothing more that evening than to have the woman dance her dreams over his. A man who understood how artifice and allure can sometimes alchemize a woman born of ordinary California earth. How, moments before the accident, red silk scarf, exposed rear wheel axle, speeding car, Isadora made an ecclesiastical date with another familiar stranger to whisk her into the promise of both pleasure and darkness. Another night too late to get up in time for breakfast.

She wishes she knew how to write stories like the one about Isadora and the one about the woman and the strawberries. She writes poems, sometimes, but has never written a poem about why people have pretty much stopped eating toast.

Her husband gets paid to write screenplays about vampires fighting zombies in Paris. Most people think all vampires live in Paris. They have been to Paris, she and her husband. Her husband called the trip a "write-off." They visited the city right before winter, but even in Paris, her husband was unable to find one strawberry éclair.

The woman who ate strawberries all winter worked in a dance hall. A "dime-a-dance girl," men paid the woman ten cents a song to pretend to desire their arms around her. The woman who ate strawberries in winter even let the tips of her peroxide curls touch the men's suit lapels. In the time of dance hall girls, what they called taxi dancers, this could cause the kind of scandal reported about in local papers. Everyone knows most stories aren't true. She hopes the story about the woman and the strawberries is not made up.

Strawberries grow all year in Florida. Most people don't know this. The woman in the story lived in New York, or maybe Paris, someplace where weather defines the season. On Spring Break of her senior year, after reading the story about the woman who loved strawberries, she took a bus to Plant City, Florida to attend the annual strawberry festival. Other places in Florida celebrate garlic and hearts of palm, which they call swamp cabbage, and even blueberries.

Each year, the Florida Strawberry Festival crowns a Strawberry Queen, a First Maid, and a Strawberry Court. The girls are usually blonde, always smiling. They have what she refers to as "cheerleader names" like Lindsey and Susan and Tori. Wearing a crown and sash becomes the logical next step. When she got off the bus, she was too late to enter the contest. She lost the strawberry shortcake eating contest, too. She tried to eat four pounds of strawberry shortcake, including whipped cream, in ten minutes. She really did try.

The woman in the story ate her strawberries suspended in a bowl of heavy cream. The woman did not bake pie or shortcake, or mash the berries with sugar until they bled a red jelly that pooled in the bottom of their bowl. To her, strawberries don't seem worth such reverence. In the story, the woman never explained why she put up with the strange smells of strange men, the hands that crept too low and the lips that inched too close, the fingers that tried to peel back her perfumed shell to crawl inside her skin.

She and her lover sit on his couch in the afternoon, ready to crawl inside each other's skin. She tells him how she was almost crowned Florida's Strawberry Queen. He is a good lover to pretend her story is true. What did your sash look like? Did you have to wear a red dress? Ride a float in a parade? She answers every question between bites of pastry. Sometimes a strawberry éclair, sometimes a Nanaimo bar, though she has never liked coconut. Her husband knows this. Her lover does not. This is a point against him.

She never feeds her lover. That is not how this works.

When she was a little girl, almost too long ago to remember, her father took her for an ice cream sundae.

"We're on a date," he said. "A date means the man pays for everything, even if you ask for extra sprinkles."

The waiter brought her sundae with a fork. Hot fudge dripped down the cold glass to pool along a paper doily. Her father waited to eat his sundae until the hot fudge deflated the vanilla scoops. The entire dessert collapsed on itself as she waited for him to feed her. Her father did not feed her. She was a big girl. She was close to knowing all the big girl things. She already knew not to ask for a spoon.

A restaurant in New York City serves the Golden Opulence Sundae. They charge $1,000. They ask you to order the dessert 48 hours in advance. Transforming dessert into opulence takes time. Madagascar vanilla bean ice cream, 23-karat edible gold leaf, gold-covered almonds, marzipan chocolate. Her husband researched the sundae in *The Guinness Book of World Records*.

"It's really not that unreasonable if what they say here is true, that you get to keep the Baccarat crystal goblet."

Sometimes he did this to her, this tone of collusion. She fell for it every time.

She told her husband before their last anniversary that she wanted to fly to New York City and share the Golden Opulence Sundae with him.

"What are you talking about?" he said.

He always did this, too, pretending to forget. Forgetting to remember. She showed him the *World Records* book, how he had dog-eared the page, underlined *Amedei Porcelana*, the Tuscan chocolate they melt into syrup to drizzle over the edible gold leaf. How he had shown interest, seemed present, aware of what she found interesting.

"I guess I wasn't paying attention." Her husband reached for her body on the couch, wove her folded arms into his. "Why don't we go on a picnic instead? Hot dogs by the lake, that cake you really like from that one bakery downtown."

"That sounds nice," she said.

Sometimes she pretends they are going on a picnic. She does not like to call him her lover.

Women who have lovers know how to coordinate accessories. They know how to buy flowers in a market. They know how to pick out eggplants but call them *aubergines*. In her mind, she watches him, her lover, count all the birds in a field. They are on a picnic, and the birds look darker than a strawberry, darker than the way her body blushes each time his fork comes near.

They serve the Golden Opulence Sundae with an 18-karat gold spoon. They do not let you keep the spoon.

In Europe, they serve dessert with a spoon. After she turned seventeen, she spent a month in Germany. Her school called this Foreign Exchange, but never told her which student they exchanged her for. In Stuttgart, even cocoa comes with a spoon. They call the drink *Heiße Schokolade.* They serve two thin packets of sugar on the side and one piece of dark chocolate. The whipped cream floating on top never really melts.

In Germany, it was easy to get a boyfriend. They loved the American girls with their American cassette tapes. Her boyfriend in Germany always asked about the time she saw Pearl Jam in concert. He kissed her once in front of the Galatea Fountain. She tried not to think about Nazis when he pressed her against the moist stone edge. Someone had spray-painted, in red, "Nazis Suck." After the kiss they walked through a forest near the fountain. Her German boyfriend tried to explain the concept of *Waldeinsamkeit.* The word translates to mean either a feeling of solitude in a forest, or forest loneliness. Foreign exchange students did not need to speak another language to travel.

She decided the long word she couldn't pronounce meant forest loneliness. Less Thoreau, more Brothers Grimm, right before the monster appears. Then she remembered how her mother once told her the monsters in fairytales live inside all of us.

"Don't you feel them moving around when you try to sleep?" her mother asked.

"Isn't that my heart?"

"That's just what everyone wants you to believe."

She wishes she had kissed her German boyfriend, just

once, deep in the forest; so deep, even the missing persons posters, the ones a consulate office fills in with their pictures and names, couldn't find them.

She loved the way her lover kissed her when she was brand new. She loved the way he kissed her when he thought she belonged to him. The secret he never knew his tongue revealed, an eternal longing to belong to someone.

She remembers asking between kisses, "Do you know that David Bowie song where he says, 'I had to phone someone so I picked on you?' But he sings it, 'you-hoo-hoo.' Is that the same reason you picked me? Because you had to pick someone?"

She loved the way he kissed her before he knew she had never really belonged to anyone.

They first slept together in a motel room in the center of their small town. Even though snow settled around other cars in the parking lot, she remembers his hair smelled like he was a child playing all day in the sun. She wanted to quit kissing and ask what he thought about being alive, right now. Their "right now," along with the "right nows" of all the world's lovers, is what eventually creates *Waldeinsamkeit.*

As a seventeen-year-old girl in the German forest she already sensed this. There had to be a tower somewhere inside those woods. Not a gingerbread house and the farsighted witch, but a tower that stores every sigh and smile and kiss and note and text and Christmas present and anniversary dinner and pet name of every relationship before it goes bad. See the plate of eggs someone fried into the shape of hearts on a long-ago Valentine's morning? See the pair of red gloves a lover lost in the snow, retrieved by her partner on the day he risked frostbite to keep her hands warm? Can't you add up all the money spent on all the hotels? Look at all that lingerie. Look at all those copies of Neruda's *Twenty Love Poems and a Song of Despair.* Look at all those mix tapes.

Will there be a subsidy if she applies to be The Keeper of the *Waldeinsamkeit*? How much is overtime? Do they hand out free turkeys at Christmas? The application asks her to fill in the names of her past lovers. One cannot be The Keeper of the *Waldeinsamkeit* without an adequate understanding of romantic pain. Committing a crime of passion earns automatic insurance benefits with a lower deductible. Being a poet is considered a pre-existing condition.

She loses track after lover four on the job application. Job applications are sometimes like this, and who she has slept with is covered under the HIPAA Act. What is love, anyway, but a fairytale?

In the fairytales she writes in her head, no one is guaranteed a happy ending. No one lets her read the stories to their children before bed. Her fairytales are full of moans and sighs and stale chocolate cake, and love letters with the best parts cut out. In the fairytales she writes in her head, she sends everyone to bed without supper, just because she can.

After she meets her lover, her characters never go to bed without supper. Not even the bad ones. He offers to take her to New York. Weekend getaway. Golden Opulence Sundae. One of those I LOVE NY t-shirts.

"You know I can't just leave. I think someone might notice."

"Good."

"No. Bad."

"If you really don't want to be with your husband anymore, why don't you just tell him?"

"Because I don't know how to tell anyone anything."

"Well, then instead of telling him, why don't you just ask?"

When she was little she knew she might go to bed without supper if she asked for ketchup. Her mother served the meatloaf plain. When she was little she also knew not to ask for a larger shoe when the man who measured her by asking her to step on a foot-shaped metal plate told her mother the wrong size. She knew not to ask if she could keep her dollhouse. Everyone in the family decided she had outgrown extra ketchup and old shoes and a house with an open front where a doll family sat around a kitchen table.

Her family gave the dollhouse and doll family to a girl too young to notice the bat and board siding, the tiny wooden shingles, the gingerbread trim. Too young to notice the teeny red felt heart she placed inside a pocket of each doll's clothing the Valentine's Day before she grew too old for what her mother called, "Such foolishness."

She gave the doll family red felt valentines because she thought making valentines was the most important thing she knew how to do. The afternoon before Valentine's Day, all those years ago, her hands cut a pile of misshapen felt offerings before they mastered the ability to fold a slice of felt so small, the fabric almost disappeared between her fingers.

Baby Doll, the smallest member of the doll family, wore a dress trimmed in yellow Dotted Swiss. Baby Doll whispered to her at night, when everyone else became ensconced in their dreams, and dolls do so love to dream, that her name was actually Dot.

"Can you please call me Dot, at least after the others go to bed?"

"No," she told Baby Doll.

"Why not?" Her yellow bib darkened from tears smaller than the red felt heart Baby Doll rubbed thin between her tiny fingers.

"Because my mother doesn't call me by the right name, either."

Brother Doll wore overalls and a red flannel shirt. He wanted to write detective books. Brother Doll spent each evening telling Baby Doll a story about a girl her age who lived in a shopping cart.

"It must be awful lonely in there." Again, Baby Doll tried to hide her tears in her bib.

"Tell me why you think that, or more specifically, why you think that you think that."

Brother Doll had just finished reading a book about Cognitive Behavioral Therapy.

"Because all the things the girl loved would fall through the holes."

Mother Doll, who she sometimes called Big Fat Momma, or Mommie Dearie, pinned her felt valentine to her kitchen apron. The apron held safe twenty-five other red hearts.

At least three times a week she pretended it was the day before Valentine's Day. At least three times a week she asked her mother for another scrap of red felt from the scrap box. At least three times a week she imagined that she was actually Baby Doll. She called herself Dot just out of Baby Doll's sensitive ears. If her father was home from work on one of the three days a week she pretended it was the day before Valentine's Day, she asked him to turn his head before she tucked a valentine inside the jacket pocket of Daddy Doll's three-piece suit. She wondered if she loved Daddy Doll more than she loved her real father. She wonders now if this is called transference.

Daddy Doll worked for a company that sold correction fluid. This meant he spent his life fixing other people's mistakes. How tedious, she thought, to spend each day erasing the past instead of living inside the present. A casual observer would call Daddy Doll successful. Such a tall house. Such tight gingerbread trim. Real balsa wood, never pressboard with those cheap, splintering edges. A matching set of dishes. Plastic groceries with hand-painted labels. A soap dispenser in the upstairs bathroom that a tiny hand could actually pump.

Did the girl her family gave her dollhouse to notice the miniature cabbage roses dancing along the kitchen wallpaper? How the knobs on the dollhouse television turned? That a parade of red felt hearts filled every empty space, from the bathtub to the fireplace mantle to the bowl of fake fruit centered on the kitchen table? She knew not to ask to keep a few of the hearts, even when the girl didn't see the little red dollops of love spilling out as her parents loaded the house into their car.

She knew not to ask for another husband when she outgrew the first one. Before he was her husband, he once won her a teddy bear at the county fair. The bear wore an orange bow around its neck. Something about the bear reminded her of fire, like maybe if she set the bear too close to the heater, his body would ignite.

The body of her lover ignites her, but that is not why she thinks she loves him. Oscar Wilde once wrote, "A kiss may ruin a human life." She thinks his mouth has ruined hers. What does it actually take to ruin a human life? In the bathtub, she wonders if Oscar Wilde meant death, or something worse. In the grime of her bathtub ring she scratches with her fingernail the ways her lover's mouth has destroyed her.

1. She prefers his mouth to her husband's mouth.
2. This means she not only prefers the way his soft, thick lips rest lightly on hers when they kiss, but also the way his lips look when he says words like "strawberry."
3. He has never compared any part of her body to a strawberry. He does not call her Strawberry.
4. Sometimes he calls her something else. She is never going to tell you what.
5. She has never blamed his mouth for all the things it calls her after the kissing.
6. She has never gone with him to a county fair because they can't go anywhere someone might see them.
7. If anyone saw them standing near each other, they would know.
8. Everything.

That night at the fair all those years ago, before he was her husband, her boyfriend ate cotton candy. It wasn't like in the movies when a couple feeds each other bursting spirals of pink, inviting fluff. Their hands felt sticky, too uncomfortable to touch each other. No one remembered to grab napkins. On the horizon, past the lights of the Ferris wheel and Tilt-a-Whirl, a mess was forming neither of them would know how to clean up. This mess was not even something close to love. This mess was something she wanted to forget.

She keeps forgetting the day of the week. She will see him again soon. He tells her he dreams she is a Russian spy. In his dreams, she is covered in body hair, even under her arms. She thinks this is a sign to quit shaving. Everything feels like a sign. Her sister says everything feeling like a sign is a symptom of temporal lobe seizures. Her sister always ruins everything.

On days she can't see him, she spends all afternoon at the grocery store. She wanders around the fruit and vegetable aisles. Under the right light she still looks thirty. "In Paris they love produce more than they love women." She thinks she heard this quote in a play, though the play did not take place in Paris. She looks up "Parisian grocery store" on the internet before each trip to the market.

Mushrooms always come up first, but of course they don't call them mushrooms. In her mind now the word resembles "champagne," or she could just be remembering something else. When she and her husband went to Paris, they ate in restaurants. They had a driver. There were no markets.

Her lover wants to take her to Paris with his profit share check. Her lover says *profit share check* and *stock portfolio* in every conversation. She tells him she already drank champagne at the top of the Eiffel Tower out of a plastic flute. La Bar Champagne. 21 euros for the pleasure. She also tells him her husband might notice. She asks him what he wants to do in Paris.

"I want to be in Paris with you."

Nothing in him wants to write poems or paint pictures. He just wants to visit Paris because, well, it's Paris. She likes not having to lie about his poems being really good, important poems or his paintings being really good, important paintings. She likes how there are no oil pastel drawings of Francis Bacon meeting Pope Francis in his apartment.

The Pope Francis would know several private, hidden things, like whether or not Notre Dame de Paris really houses Jesus' Crown of Thorns. The Francis Bacon would know several private, hidden things, like whether or not Jesus' Crown of Thorns is worth visiting when the resident priests parade the filigreed tube full of what look like pine needles through the church on the first Friday of each month. On posters outside the main entrance, Notre Dame calls this "The Veneration." This is not why he wants to visit Paris.

"I want to see you seeing Paris," he says.

"I want to see you tomorrow instead of Friday. My husband will be home early. We need to shop for groceries. We need to walk the dog."

"But you don't have a dog."

"The kind of woman who has a husband and a lover should also have a dog. A dog makes me a sympathetic character. Women who read this won't turn against me as fast if I have a dog, so in the next draft start me off with a pug. Everyone loves pugs, with those noses and their impossibly curly tails."

"Okay. In the next draft, you can have a dog, but only if we get to visit Paris."

"I can only be gone for an afternoon."

"Well then," he says, "we better make the most of it."

Gâteau au Fromage Blanc. She scans for recipes online. *Gâteau* . . . cake. *Fromage au Blanc* . . . white cheese? One recipe says she can substitute farmer cheese, but she doesn't know where to buy farmer cheese. She promised to bake him a French dessert. An afternoon is not enough time to visit Paris, but almost enough time to bake something creamy and foreign. Her husband works nights.

Her husband also works days and weekends. Her husband tells her he works nights and days and weekends so she can spend forty-five dollars at the gourmet market downtown buying the ingredients to make *Gâteau Fromage au Blanc.* One lemon, extra-large, organic Meyer if they are in season. Four eggs, brown. (The recipe does not call for this.) One pie crust. One tub of *crème fraîche.* (Please do not substitute sour cream.) Two tubs of *fromage blanc.* (Substitute whole milk ricotta, but only this once.) The fragrant insides of one slashed vanilla bean.

The cake does not turn out the way it tasted in Paris, almost as if every *patisserie* in the city harnesses the supernatural ability to mix milk, flour, and butter into an epiphany.

This is my body.

This is my blood.

This is how I would taste if someone baked me into a cake.

Her husband finds her kneeling on the kitchen floor. She eats great hunks of warm *Gâteau au Fromage Blanc* with her hands. Next to her sits a green book with gold-edged pages. She pretends to read poems from the book; big, important poems with lines like, "I do not talk about the beginning or the end."

All she and her lover talk about is the beginning and the end. With her husband, she talks about bills and refilling the pepper mill and whether or not her cousin

Jane is looking too old to wear leather miniskirts. All she and her lover talk about is the beginning and end of everything, from the metamorphosis of a caterpillar to whether or not the Big Bang Theory will ever be proven to how, as each month passes, both of their bodies are dying. They both know *Gâteau au Fromage Blanc* will not make anything better but, after her husband leaves the kitchen, she stands from the book of poems and makes another cake. This cake she saves for her lover. When no one is looking, she sheds one tear into the cake batter. When no one is looking, she pricks her finger with a carving knife and squeezes into the batter one red drop.

This is my body.

This is my blood.

She sets the oven timer and waits for the cake to leave its scent upon the room.

She met her lover standing in someone else's kitchen. He changed her life in one sentence.

"I am supposed to take the coats and put them in the back bedroom."

She handed him her coat at the party.

"I am also supposed to point you towards the drinks. Most people are requesting martinis, but I don't like vodka or gin."

"My husband likes both," she said, "but he is at home finishing a deadline."

"Silly man," he said, "to miss a whole evening without you. Look how much you are changing by the minute. When you get home, he won't even recognize you."

"Who are you and why are you in my house?" her husband said hours later.

"Don't be weird. I told you I might be late."

"I will seriously call the cops if you don't either explain yourself, or get out of here."

"Come on, you know parties can drain me for days. It's like you said in that one script. Cocktail parties really are portals to hell. Even calling one purgatory is too kind."

She unzipped and stepped out of her red satin dress in front of her husband. The action did not feel sexual. When her warm body hit the cold air, she felt overexposed. She asked her husband to remove his clothes.

"You mean right here, in the living room?"

Silly man, she thought, *look how much you have missed out on this evening. Look how much I have changed.*

Sometimes she worries about changing too much in between the times she sees her lover. Will he notice a grey hair, or a blemish? That chicken pox scar on her left shoulder? She hopes to become the woman he thinks she is. That idiom about living up to his "tall order," though she is only average. 5'9" in heels. Around him she takes off her shoes. He never notices her pedicure. So many other parts garner his attention.

"You remind me of Paris," he says.

"But you have never been to Paris."

"I assume it's nothing like what anyone thinks it is. Am I right?"

"You are right," she says.

"Then you remind me of Paris. Isn't the city nice this time of year?"

She hands him a large wedge of *Gâteau au Fromage Blanc,* but she just calls it cheesecake. He is jealous she has already seen Paris. "Yes," she says, "Paris is nice this time of year."

"Remember when we walked over to *Île Saint-Louis* to have ice cream?"

"Of course!" she says between mouthfuls of eggy, lemony cake. They sit on an old wool blanket thrown over his living room rug. "But they call it *glace,* and we didn't know what that word meant or how to pronounce it."

(They have never even gone grocery shopping together, or out to dinner, or talked over a cup of coffee in the small town where they live. Forget about Paris.)

"What do you remember?" she asks him.

"Come here," he says, "and let me show you."

They walk towards the bedroom. She winds the alarm clock beside his bed. He likes to pretend he is old-fashioned and prefers a real clock over red digital numbers. Each afternoon they see each other, she winds his alarm clock to keep track of when she needs to be home. She calls this stage setting, the ability to turn the affair into something more romantic by their shared over-awareness of passing time.

"This time why don't you set it?" he asks.

She watches him undress by the window. She doesn't think anything good, or bad, about his body. "So we're timing ourselves? Is that our new game?"

"No. We are going to crawl into my bed and dream. Meet me by the Seine in a half hour."

She doesn't end up finding him in a dream of Paris. She agrees to meet him the next day for lunch one town over. Her lover tries to convince her they would make a beautiful baby. He tells her this in the only restaurant where they know no one will see them. He orders hot spinach dip. He knows she doesn't like hot spinach dip. After the waitress walks away, he tells her about a vision he had the night before about having a baby with her.

"Don't put images in my mind that will never happen."

"Would you really never consider having a baby with me?"

The hot spinach dip sits untouched on the table. The last thing she wants is to get pregnant. Before she sleeps with him each time, she excuses herself to his small bathroom.

Running the water to mimic the sound of washing up,

the sound of teeth brushing, she prays to each fertility god and goddess she memorized off the internet to not come anywhere near.

"Get away from me, Saint Gerard," she whispers near the running faucet. "You too, Kokopelli. And back off, Aphrodite." She does not care that her reverse invocations would hurt his feelings. This is a sign that she should put on her clothes and leave. She doesn't leave.

He yells from the bedroom, "Hurry up so I can tell you about the cherry blossom éclairs I read about. They make them in France and I want to learn how to make them for you."

Her sister tells her éclairs only come in chocolate. She also tells her to quit talking about Mary Janes.

"What does one have to do with the other?" she asks.

"I don't know, but you seem to bring them both up a lot. Is there something going on with you? Like one of those secrets I don't really want to know about, but that you should probably tell me? I bet you don't even know what a Mary Jane is."

"Of course I know. Don't you remember?"

The old-fashioned taffy with the peanut butter center, the yellow wrapping, the fat red stripe, its namesake stamped in black on each piece. Mary Jane's bonnet. Mary Jane's own name written on her very own dress. She wonders if a scientist somewhere, probably in France, won an award proving how eating certain types of candy can cure depression. When she's away from him, all she wants to do is to suck on something sweet. Her sister calls this a personality disorder. Her sister calls this an affair. Her sister tells her to study *The Diagnostic and Statistical Manual of Mental Disorders.*

"There are over four hundred different kinds," her sister says.

No store near them sells Mary Janes. She wants to pick out the candy in person instead of ordering it through the mail. She wants her lover to bring her a box of Mary Janes without having to ask.

"Ordering my candy off a computer strips it of every last bit of myth. How can you not understand that?" she asks her sister.

"You can't keep turning everything into a myth. Your husband. Your lover. Candy you haven't eaten since grade school. Remember how it always got caught in your teeth?"

She wonders if the woman who ate strawberries in winter ever felt seeds caught between her teeth. Dancing with strange men while she tried to pick seeds from her mouth with no one noticing must've been the loneliest feeling in the world.

Once her college English professor asked her why her poems centered on her fear of being alone. He asked her to stay after school. More like he invited her to wait in a private room for him to blow in like a Nabokov character, every part of his body an innuendo of fumbling tweed.

A Hershey bar fell from his pocket. She remembers this, and wonders why he didn't bring something more expensive. Was she not worth better chocolate? In a private study area far past his classroom, he offered to dissect her schoolgirl poems.

"If these ever get published, kiddo, they'll crucify you in the press for that one piece."

He called her poems "pieces." This thrilled her to no end.

"Which one?"

"The piece where the concentration camp victim looks forward to a visit from her captor just so that she 'Can pretend for a moment he is coming to pick her up for a date and there will be real napkins and red wine conversations.' You really gotta quit writing about Nazis, kiddo. We're nowhere near World War Two, and you are nowhere near Jewish."

"I'm half. On my mother's side. Every girl adores a *Stechschritt.*"

He smiled.

In her dreams, she still polishes the toes of the German soldiers' boots. She calls out names that sound German, but are probably Russian. She never feels guilty because she has been in combat most of her life.

Her teacher halved the chocolate bar. She broke her half into six even pieces. She always followed guidelines. His tweed limbs never reached out to feed her a tiny rectangle of cloying, milky sweetness. He told her he had diabetes, that eating sugar could kill him. This meant his wife never allowed chocolate in the house.

"So we will never tell anyone we met like this, okay? I'm sure my number one special student would never want to get me in trouble."

"Am I your number one special girl?" she asks her lover.

"Are you trying to piss me off right now?"

She tells him, "No! I really just want to know."

"Yes, you are my number one special girl, but I am not your number one special guy, so if you insist on humiliating me by asking that, you better think again."

"Okay. What are you doing on Valentine's Day?"

"I assume you will be spending it with your husband."

"He'll be out of town. Can I spend it with you?"

On Valentine's Day, she asks her lover to drive her to the grocery store. It is the kind of store that also has a pharmacy and a bank. On Valentine's Day, they remove the desk where customers fill out withdrawal and deposit slips. The store manager replaces the desk with a low table. Behind the table a man wearing a chef's *toque*, she has never seen a *toque* in the middle of the day, in the middle of a store, stands behind a large pot of melted chocolate. The man dips strawberries the size of plums into the chocolate. He packages the berries in containers that look like the same boxes high school corsages come in.

"I think the berries are pretty enough to pin to a dress," she says. "Don't you?"

He doesn't offer to buy her any. He is mad that she is not really his valentine.

"Can I be your valentine, at least for tonight?" she asks him.

"I guess."

They drive to every kitchen store in town on the hunt for a melon baller. He wants to show her what he learned in culinary school about fruit carving. He was a line cook in a fish restaurant before becoming a stockbroker. He keeps calling his secret special technique "Food Garnish." This makes her think of parsley, and those lemons that one fancy steakhouse wraps in yellow cheesecloth tied with a green onion so diners can squeeze the juice onto halibut without fear of choking on seeds.

"If you liked the chocolate strawberries, wait until you see what I can do with a melon baller."

She doesn't tell him the word "baller" sounds too sexual, or athletic, or some alarming combination of both.

When they were new to each other, he picked her up at midnight while her husband continued to dream. Her husband never knew she was missing as she crept away from their bed to lace up her shoes. This meant she had already been gone for a very long time.

When they were new to each other, she and the man she is supposed to pass in the grocery store and pretend she doesn't know, whether or not they both stop to watch a chef wearing a *toque* dip strawberries the size of plums in a pot of melted chocolate, took her out for hot fudge sundaes at the all-night diner and let them melt without eating many bites.

They existed inside happiness, like the moment in a Springsteen song before everything goes bad.

Then everything went bad.

Her husband takes her out for gelato. She doesn't answer her lover's texts. She wants to pretend he doesn't exist. She wants to pretend she doesn't love him so she can go back to being married. This kind of pretending makes her feel alone, and sad. People around her ask for tastes of *stracciatella* and *zabaione* by pointing to the flavors no one wants to mispronounce.

A girl ordering at the gelato counter has a strawberry the size of a palm tattooed on the back of her right calf. She wonders if the girl's big red tattoo hides a birthmark. She thinks her lover would like the girl and her birthmark.

He likes the bump on her nose because it looks like someone broke it. She thinks he has convinced himself that she is broken and needs him to put her back together.

He bites her when they are together. His teeth always bring blood to the surface of her skin. As a couple, they never call these marks "strawberries." What they do isn't what couples who go steady in old movies call "necking." Streams of blood pool in her collarbone.

Later, when she crawls into bed with her husband, he asks about the blood, the bites.

"It's nothing," she always says. "I've just been away for a while. I will be back soon. Don't worry."

"What were you out doing?" her husband asks between slow, sleepy breaths.

"I don't really remember."

Her husband turns from her in bed.

She and her lover feed each other cupcakes in bed. Six at a time, snuggled in a small white box from a bakery without pink boxes. The baker always thinks they are going to a party. The baker says they must know a lot of people, but they don't know anyone. There is already a glacier forming between them when they tuck themselves in. They call the imminent threat of snow nothing more than a flavor, vanilla, but when he touches her, she shivers. Almost like a lighthouse, she sees the end coming, shines the warning signal, but her lover cannot see it, yet.

They never watch the same kind of movie. She likes movies where rich girls in revolutionary France bite into cream puffs before tossing out the leftovers. She likes Marie Antoinette dancing in her movie to the same song she danced to in high school, before boys and girls dreamed of feeding each other cupcakes. They call this an anachronism. A detail out of place, the punch line of a joke told generations back. She hopes they are not like this.

When she was in high school, only mothers made cupcakes, and only for parties, and only sometimes. Now she always picks chocolate. He always picks white, the boat of their romance chugging towards its iceberg.

In bed he feeds her bites too big to swallow without choking.

"Quit pretending you are choking," he says.

She loses her breath on his turn. He nips her fingers when he bites down.

He tells her he can't see her anymore over a chocolate-dipped cannoli in a cafe downtown. This is the first time they have ever gone to a cafe together. She is just starting to consider leaving her husband to be with him. He has waited three years. Is tired of waiting, though when they first met, he told her he would wait a lifetime.

This has been coming for a long time. She can't be what he needs.

He wants to die.

She wants to die.

He wants to kill her.

She wants him to kill her.

They break the brittle cookie shell in half. Out comes all the cream.

This is my body.

Through tears she jokes about Communion, how each new Pope is just like the last Pope. He says something must happen when they walk through the Room of Tears.

This makes her think of the Hall of Justice. She asks, "Superman, right? Remember the old cartoon where he shoots his web towards a man formed from bees?"

"Did you hear anything I just said, about how this will be the last time we will ever see each other? That I don't want to see you ever again? That I don't want you to call me ever again? If you ever call me again, I just might die."

The man formed from bees wasn't really a man at all, but a colony, a brigade, a cohesive unit commandeering a war even their inborn sweetness refused to stop.

He asks her to stop crying. "It isn't the end of the world until it's the end of the world," he says before paying the check. He leaves her alone at a big cafe table. Every man she's known has asked her to stop crying. Tears make men want to jump off tall buildings instead of leaping them in a single bound.

A scientist does not win an award proving this.

KITTY PARTY

Junie made photocopies of the flyer with her picture on it after she went missing. The man who showed her how to use the machine didn't recognize her from the flyer as he fanned the papers before putting the flyers in a box. Neither did the downtown store owners when she asked to hang the flyers in their front windows. By then, with her disappearance dominating the national news and her fan base growing nightly, Junie's plain, middle-aged face left no impression as she wandered through town.

It didn't really surprise Junie that she turned invisible on her fortieth birthday. She had begun to disappear a few years earlier, her already-thinning hair discernible to men on the prowl for a mate; her lips only full now with lipstick and liner, which she seldom wore. Her eyes wrinkled around the edges no matter how many previous years of religious sunglass wearing. She had never felt particularly attractive in her body, but becoming invisible?

It didn't really surprise her any more than organizing

the first kitty party in her neighborhood all those months ago, a transplant from a larger town who now lived in a cul-de-sac. To lure other women in the neighborhood, she painted the front door red and placed two large baskets of bleeding hearts on either side of the porch. A fresh start, she promised her husband. *And I'll promise to never look back, if you promise, too.* But as hard as she and Marcus tried, nothing in the new house looked new, the same bed and the same dining table and the same pink couch in a different living room, the couch still so overstuffed it hurt anyone's back who pressed very long against the lighter pink row of bolster pillows.

She missed her twenties, that old cliché of no bodily aches or pains combined with the potential around each corner of every day to meet someone new. Newness now involved inviting new women to the new house she kept with her old husband. As a group these women, with overstuffed couches of their own, first took to decoupage to forget about becoming invisible. After three months at the new house, Junie refinished a Goodwill desk with a collage of antique seed packets. When the others came to her house every few weeks for a girls' night, everyone took turns hosting, they admired her flat edges, complimented her lack of bubbles rippling beneath the packets. What a world to live in at forty, commended for the ability to apply glue.

"It's simple. I just take a knife to the pieces that won't

stay where they are supposed to."

Did she sense that weird feeling from the group each time she spoke, or had the hospital made her paranoid? It was supposed to do the opposite, cure her of the desire to follow home just about any man who paid her even the slightest attention. This could be a smile from a Starbucks barista, a nod from a grocery clerk. After the age of thirty-five, Junie believed the average American female should be forgiven for most unorthodox behavior, as long as nobody got hurt. It was the hormones, right? Some days wanting to sleep with any warm body that came near, other days wanting to lounge around in pajamas with a jar of hot fudge, alone. The pharmaceutical companies needed to get behind this, invent a drug, preferably cocoa-based, to ease once-young, fecund beings into never again being asked to go to the front of the grocery line or the backseat of a car.

Marcus knew Junie meant nothing by any of it, would never actually touch one of the men she followed home, let alone take their, or her, clothes off. "It's just a habit," he'd always say, "like eating a piece of candy after dinner every night."

"I do that, the candy thing, for the flavonoids. Please don't call it a habit."

Sometimes, with no one interesting enough to follow at night, Junie got on a bus. It wasn't like anyone noticed her as she sat in the dark, sucking on mint after mint until a whole pack disappeared from her purse. Once she got to her destination, the end of the bus line, she'd turn around and come right back. Some nights she slipped back into bed before Marcus's alarm went off at six, other times she greeted him after his next day's work with dinner, her peace offering. He never mentioned her missed hours as long as she remembered to serve the steak hot and the accompanying salad cold.

Before the years of hospital stays, the gently forced therapy, Junie knew she followed men into their homes, late at night while they slept, because she was addicted to pretending to be those other men. Strong, deep-voiced, with the power to demand the correct order at the Starbucks drive-thru on their way to managing companies with too many employees to track. Men who would never become invisible, no matter how old or wrinkled or shamed on the internet for groping another young intern.

Junie would stand at the foot of the desired person's bed. She never touched herself. Her compulsion wasn't sexual. She hoped this constant, careful observing would help her choose an identity of her own to settle into someday. *Maybe in the next life*, she always thought. Something more than existing as Marcus's disappearing wife.

What's the real harm in finding myself, she reasoned for so many months during her involuntary confinement that the doctors gave up trying to figure out a better explanation and always ended up releasing her back into the same "destructive" routine.

Yes, her behavior was illegal, and irresponsible, and just plain weird, might even get her killed if the wrong person woke as she stood before him, swaying in the dark to the music of silence, she and the stranger, beloved for the way his silence unburdened those thoughts that twisted around a root so deep, they never left her brain, but Junie promised in this new town to not give in to her urges. She vowed to join a circle of women, be it a book club, sewing club, cooking club. Maybe the distraction could take away her thoughts of leaving Marcus to follow the next intriguing man, or bus route, and keep going, and never stop.

In a den on another floor Marcus drank beer while the neighborhood women invaded his house with too much floral perfume and too many purses with nowhere to set them. Her husband could still sort of see her, even though the grocery clerks, younger women included, stared past her now at check-out time. The true purgatory of middle age, it would take years before everyone started to see her again once they began to ask the back of her gray hair if she needed help carrying her groceries to the car.

A row of gray and black and brown handbags lined the hallway if Marcus dared use the bathroom. The high laughter of too many women in one small kitchen below sounded more like hyenas than neighbors. Junie hated the cacophony of women together, too, but she knew what would happen if she messed up again.

Decoupage dates failed to keep the women's interest, so they decided as a group to replace the cutting and gluing with the dice game Bunco. At Junie's turn to host, again she impressed the women with her rented card tables and her appetizers.

Maggs picked a square, white object off a flowered plate. "Is this a real boiled egg?"

She sold real estate, same as Junie. They competed for listings the way two teenage girls compete for the same boy's attention in a calculated series of insults masked as vague, mostly confusing compliments.

"I found a vintage egg cuber online. They used to make them for bridge parties. Once I stick the cloves in," Junie took the egg out of Maggs's perfectly manicured hand to mark each side with different, evenly spaced black dots, "it really does look like a die."

"A die?" Maggs's ten red nails clicked against each other in a quick and futile struggle to find something else to clutch. "I knew I could learn a lot from someone like you, who cares about more interesting things than how they look."

"Like dice but only one, since we're playing a dice game tonight."

On a tray Junie arranged a row of toasted bread slices cut into rectangles and spread with cream cheese. She tried not to sink into that familiar ugly feeling as she added to each toast card suits and numbers punched from red and green peppers with another vintage kitchen tool. This sort of busywork almost quieted the thoughts she never shared with Marcus, or the doctors. Dark thoughts only other women born not quite pretty enough understand. Women destined from birth to disappear.

"Pretty impressive." Maggs watched the party platter grow before her on the counter. "You must have a lot of extra time. Who knows how many hours I waste each week on stupid shit like putting on make-up before work."

"I don't have more time than anyone else. I just love details. That's probably the reason we moved here. It's too hard in an apartment to pay attention to details."

"Really? You'd think it'd be easier."

Junie ignored Maggs to arrange wedges of cheddar cheese into yellow-orange fans like a handful of cards. "Have you played Bunco together before?"

"Only once or twice before you moved here. Angela got the idea from a magazine. Being the wife of a dentist means she's the only one who still reads them. I thought it sounded easier than hauling around all the craft supplies. Everyone's only agreed to play because of the chance to win money."

"Why don't we just throw a kitty party?"

"Whatever that is sounds naughty."

Angela and Clarisse let themselves in after ringing the

doorbell a few times while Junie removed the red and green hearts and diamonds from the cream cheese toasts. She did not want to show any weakness to the group. Even a slight mistake, like a change in party plans her appetizers didn't immediately catch up to, might be enough to get kicked out of this social circle. This new town only organized its older women into a few circles. From what Junie could tell, this was the best one. She needed to focus on something besides her vanishing self. She missed watching strange men sleep more than she wanted to admit.

It had nothing to do with Marcus, or his abilities to be a husband. He wasn't a bad husband, as far as husbands go, Marcus with the eyes too dark to reveal much of what he thought about after work, on the weekends when he puttered around the house, the yard, her body, without ever accomplishing much. It was just hard not to resent every man, sometimes. The way they all made her feel like she had to change somehow to hold their interest. Each time over the years that she tried to improve herself for him, Marcus just told her to make friends. Develop a life beyond him. Go to parties. Throw parties of her own.

The women stared at her when Junie threw out the kitty party idea in a way she hoped sounded noncommittal, maybe even a little jokey.

You never grow out of the feeling, therapy or not. Do they like me? Wouldn't it be easier to run away and start over as someone else? I'm sure they all follow each other on social media. I don't have anything interesting enough to post on Instagram. I could've posted my square eggs. I paid a lot of money for the cuber, but if we aren't playing a dice game, they are already passé.

Junie made her pitch while the circle of women gathered around the small kitchen chewing their cream cheese toast. The plate of square boiled eggs hid in her fridge behind a bowl of fruit salad she'd sprinkled with lemon juice to keep the bananas from browning, in case anyone opened the door. An honest assessment of her looks told Junie she was the least attractive in the new group of women, which meant every other thing in her orbit must be the most beautiful, even boiled eggs.

She said, "Each month one of us gets to keep the kitty, and the rest of us contribute any amount we want. A kitty is just a fancy way of saying a communal pot of money. I read about them online. Women throw the parties all over India and Pakistan."

"Which is very different from anything going on here."

"Some people give five dollars, some twenty or more, but one of us each month keeps it. And we are under no obligation to share what we plan to do with the kitty. In fact, it's probably best to keep it to ourselves."

Marie, one of two women in the group with a designer handbag, a perfect face, and those furry Gucci tiger slippers Junie fought herself not to steal right off her feet, said, "At the most that will give us only a few hundred dollars."

"If we're lucky," someone answered.

Junie wanted to run her hands across the slipper fur as Marie said, "That's what my mom used to call mad money."

"Not even enough to spend on a shopping trip."

"Maybe a nice dinner out?"

Maggs pushed the fan of cheese wedges back into a solid stack. She asked Junie for an avocado to top her piece of toast, as if everyone in the circle could afford daily, ripe avocados. *These women are spoiled, even as they all vanish,* she thought. She arranged thin-sliced prosciutto on a tray next to a counter covered in various foreign brands of sparkling water she bought at the gourmet market. How could she forget avocados?

"We don't really keep avocados as a staple. They always go bad so fast."

Angela pretended to eat her small plate of food by rubbing the cream cheese onto a cocktail napkin. "There's an art to picking out the right ones, but it's not a big deal."

Her tone alerted Junie that yes, in fact, not providing avocados in the cul-de-sac was the biggest of deals, one that had the potential to become a heated text chain if she didn't take control.

"If a few hundred dollars doesn't sound like a good incentive . . . " She could do so much with the money.

Order more kitchen supplies, invest in a really good zester, save for avocados. " . . . we could make each kitty something more exciting?"

"Like what?" Maggs stood nearest to the kitchen island sink. She also scraped the cream cheese off her toast only to lick the goop out of the underside of her long red nails.

"We could collect for charity?" said a woman Junie didn't know well.

This group already donated to every local charity, and a few of the well-known nationals. Some gave books to every Little Free Library in town, others rescued older dogs from the local shelter. Junie felt positive one of the women in the circle, Miss Furry Slippers, might donate enough money during the next election to bring a Democrat back to power.

Junie passed around a second tray of cream cheese toasts. She motioned for everyone to move to the living room. "Or we could focus on more personal things. Something one of us secretly desires. Someone one of us secretly hates."

"I never think about things that way."

"Me, either," Clarisse said. She cleared her throat. To Junie she sounded like she was lying. "But it is very intriguing."

The women spoke in newly hushed tones around the pink couch while Junie toasted more bread, her toaster oven barely keeping up as the group collectively decided to forgo the pretense of eating and actually eat. As they gathered around the coffee table, someone burped while another asked for ketchup. After a few more rounds of tray passing, Marie pretended to call for a toast by hitting a plastic fork against her plastic champagne glass. She laughed.

(Note to self, no more plastic ever again. I know when someone is making fun of me.)

"There's this guy at the gym who really bugs me. He never touches me, or gets too close or anything, but he gives me that look. You know, like he's undressing me with his eyes."

"Always so dramatic." Maggs spoke partially under her breath, though the women all knew the stare Marie described. "At this age I'd kill for someone to look at me that way again."

"You look great for your age, Maggs."

"But I'd love to go back to the days when I looked great, period."

"Maybe lay off the cream cheese?" Marie set down her empty plate. Out of a small porcelain bowl closest to her she plucked a handful of peanut M&Ms. "My wish is to have the guy stop showing up at my gym. I'd go somewhere else, but why should I have to run away when he's the creep?" She turned to Junie. "And I never thought of putting candy in bowls at a party, Junie-June. Wouldn't it be fabulous if they matched your couch? What color are we calling it, again?"

Junie made a mental note to visit that one store downtown where you could buy candy by the color. "Right now we call it pink, but I'm sure we can think of something better. And this is the sort of idea I was talking about, each of us using our kitty to accomplish something important, like removing an obvious predator from the local gym."

"But you just met us," Angela said. "How do you know Marie's even telling the truth?"

"Because I believe her." Junie sat on the pink couch. She made another mental note to look at paint samples online.

The others drew closer, circling like girls at a kiddie birthday party poring over the birthday girl's much-envied presents.

Maggs jumped up to grab her wallet from the row of purses in the hallway. "How much money do we each throw in to make things happen?"

"That's the beauty of it." Marie dangled one of her furry slippers off the foot of her crossed leg. What Junie wouldn't give for one of those slippers. Beautiful, taupe lambswool edging a bright, growling tiger. A month's rent for a slipper. *Or I could follow you home tonight. I'm not opposed to following a woman. I'll wait until you tuck yourself in bed next to your husband and then I will just . . .* "These parties aren't about money. They're about solidarity." Marie made purposeful, lingering eye contact with Junie. "Right now, we all agree to make a formal complaint about gym guy. By the next party, we'll know if it worked."

The women exhaled loudly, most rolled their eyes. As if complaining would change a thing, especially with the burgeoning fall of their cleavage, the small pool of lax skin around their elbows in short summer sleeves. Some shrugged off the suggestion while others stared at their empty plates, or texted their husbands to let them know they'd be home soon. What are a group of women supposed to think about the power of their voices to change anything? Still, Junie felt whole in a way she had never felt before. Whole as she made small talk with the others about what to binge watch on Netflix. Whole when she reunited the ladies with their handbags at the end of the evening. The plan was set in motion to oust the gym guy, Richard Something, as soon as possible, though how did Marie know his name if they had never spoken?

Junie felt a little less whole as she purposefully stepped on the back tuft of brown fur on Marie's left Gucci shoe, but even more alive when she cleaned up, after everyone promised to follow through with the plan and drove away. No one left one piece of toast, or non-matching M&M, for her to either snack on or throw away. From her laptop she pulled up photos of pink paint samples, held a bolster pillow to the screen. Rose Mist. Apple Blossom. Piglet. Carnation.

Junie called Marie's gym a place for "pretty people." Through a large picture window next to the front parking lot, she saw rows of toned bodies running and lifting weights and turning two thick battle ropes into undulating black snakes with the fire of their mighty biceps. She worked out sporadically, sometimes after indulging in too many Duncan Hines microwaved coffee mug cakes she sneaked (while Marcus slept) at 1am, the loneliest time in the cul-de-sac. When Junie did work out, it was never very hard or for very long, she went to that place on the other side of town with no mirrors and no judgment about her slight paunch and large, soft breasts crammed into an oversized T-shirt.

The specimens behind this window stoked a feeling of jealous inadequacy. Heat flushed her body. Her thighs, rubbing together beneath her skirt, chafed ever so imperceptibly as she adjusted herself in the front seat. It didn't take long to recognize the man Marie wanted out. Inside the gym Junie watched him, Richard Somebody, make eye contact with every young woman who flounced by. Was that the silver flash of a belly ring on a concave stomach near his face as he did preacher curls on a weight bench? Didn't he stick his tongue out a little?

When Junie sought out the front desk manager, she blocked the fact that Richard Somebody also made eye contact with every older woman, and older and younger man, who walked in. Some of their abs ended up being close to his face, too. Maybe he was a salesman, or a lawyer? Or maybe he was more like her than anyone she'd met, a semi-decent person who questioned the daily machinations of life? In fact, when she thought about it, he had even smiled at her. Nobody said kitty parties were easy.

"Excuse me, but that man over there," Junie turned to point at Richard. He waved like he knew her. "Every time I come in here he makes me feel uncomfortable."

A teen sitting behind the front desk flexed his pecs beneath a tank top at least four sizes too small. He smelled like sweat. Young, musky, almost piney.

"I don't remember seeing you in here before." He didn't look up.

"How would you know without looking at me? I'm in here all the time." Junie nodded at a blonde woman becoming thinner by the minute, her treadmill cranked to the fastest running speed. The woman, twenty years her junior, ignored her. "I must come when you aren't working."

"Sorry, but I don't recognize you."

"Is it part of your job to recognize everyone who works out here?"

"I have a good memory, for people worth remembering." The boy typed on a computer, again without looking up. He wore a shiny whistle around his neck. Junie wondered if pretty men worried about being followed home the way pretty women must worry. "Our members need more than one complaint before we ask them to forfeit their membership, unless they do something completely inappropriate."

Completely inappropriate? The boy manager reminded Junie of all the other young boys in her orbit who couldn't see her. Grocery baggers who packed her bananas on top of her eggs, boys who never gave her the correct order at coffee drive-thrus, restaurant bussers who cleared away every younger woman's dirty plates before they considered cleaning her table.

"Well," Junie turned from the desk to stare at Richard, "that man over there, last week after my workout he followed me to my car and exposed himself. He was getting ready to touch it, I'm sure, but I started screaming until he ran away."

With no further questions, the young boy stormed towards Richard, pretended to grab his towel, drenched in older man sweat and hanging on a bench next to the one he still curled his large biceps over. The manager made a motion towards Junie, then towards his own crotch. Laughter filled both of their bodies until neither man, nor boy, acted like they knew how to stop.

Once Richard composed himself enough to finish his workout and leave the gym, Junie decided to follow him. Maybe not all the way home yet, since it was daylight and everyone might be watching. If Marcus found out he would call her stupid, reckless, disappointing. He would accuse her of fucking things up all over again, in this new town. But he would never find out.

At what felt like a safe distance from Richard and his car Junie yelled, "You made my friend feel like an object!"

His pale skin reddened. He threw his gym bag in the trunk without turning to look at her.

"You can ignore me all you want, but we're all sick of being treated this way!"

Richard turned towards her, took a few steps closer. His muscles protruded under a large blue tank top in a way Junie would describe as inauspicious. The air either all left her lungs, or filled up her body too quickly. Junie's breath squeezed out in a weak wheeze as she tried ordering him to back away. He stared past her like he almost couldn't see her at all. Junie thought she smelled Richard Somebody's diminishing testosterone when he stood so close.

Richard spoke to a spot above Junie's head. "Listen, I don't know who you are, but you need to stop following me."

"Can you see me? I mean, really see me?"

"Honestly, it's all a blur. It has been this whole time."

"I'm Marie's friend. Junie Springs? I'm sure she's mentioned me?"

"You don't look like a woman that belongs in that group. They're a lot more put together than you, and mean."

Typical, a man covered in sweat, pit stains larger than dinner plates, judging the fact that Junie didn't like makeup, mostly because she could never get it to go on right the first time. She jutted her chin forward like the models recommended doing in photographs to erase a middle-age double chin.

"I'm her new friend. I moved here last year."

"Wait, I bet you're the one who goes over the top on your parties. I think she told me they all call you Dumpy Martha."

"Who's that?"

"You know, a homely version of Martha Stewart. I told you those women are mean."

"At least you're admitting you know Marie. I don't know what she said about me, but she told all of us you're a pervert."

"I broke up with Marie last week. Her husband works out here, too, and it started to get a little weird. Now if you'd just step away so I can get in my car?"

"And when it's my turn to host girls' night, I throw excellent parties, by the way."

"I'm sure you do." Richard spoke in the opposite direction of Junie's voice.

"If you can't see me, how can you see her? We've got to be close in age?"

"My policy's always been to aim for the good parts and

hope for the best."

Junie noticed Richard left his windows rolled down as he zoomed out of the parking lot into the afternoon heat.

Marie threw the next party. Her house, a mansion, really, sat in the hills between a pine forest and the town park. This meant cherry blossoms decorated her yard in white and pink every spring, and by Christmas she found the best tree to cut down, practically in her own backyard.

"Richard was pretty pissed you tried to get him thrown out of the club. Isn't that funny?"

"Funny?"

Junie refused to try an M&M from the little porcelain bowls spread around Marie's kitchen and living room in shades of blue and silver to match her décor. She knew Marie didn't even like chocolate.

"You really are dear, Junie-June, to protect my honor."

Marie rattled around two M&Ms in her palm like she was playing a game and it was her turn to roll. Maggs wandered back and forth between the kitchen island and the dining room table. Two of everyone's house could fit inside Marie's, but no one complained.

"We all agreed to get rid of Richard? It was your kitty?"

Junie felt like she wore the wrong outfit again. Marcus made her promise not to take out another credit card to keep up with the rest of them, but she did find a place online, a company with an obvious Chinese name, to order a knock-off copy of Marie's furry slippers. She moved towards a large silver tray of drinks without shuffling after she noticed a tuft of brown fur had fallen off the back of one slipper to scatter about the sun-dappled room like something cheap and unwanted. When she bent to pick up the shed fur in hopes of hiding it in her purse, the tuft separated into hundreds of tiny, scratchy hairs. Remnants of some unknown animal Junie tried to blow away before rubbing the hairs on her pants. Hairs stuck in her mouth when she succumbed to a handful of blue and silver M&M's.

"You see, Junie-June, Richard and Marie have had this back-and-forth thing for years. None of us try to get involved anymore."

"So he really can still see us?"

"What are you talking about, Junie-June?"

By the third time someone called her that, she knew the women would forever know her by a nickname she already abhorred.

"How it's the same, whether I go to the grocery store or out to lunch or grab coffee on the way home. No one notices me anymore. And I don't mean because I'm not as attractive as some. It's more than that. I'm becoming invisible. And I'm being serious."

"Junie-June, you're very sweet," with the red tip of her nail Maggs pulled a brown hair off of Junie's pink lipstick, "but I think you're overreacting."

She paced with the feeling of hair still glued to her lips. "None of you think the world treats you different than it did, like, ten years ago?"

Angela said, "I just thought everyone got more into themselves because of social media?"

"Next time I'll be sure to let you know who I'm fucking before I send you out into the world, love. Just think of the thing with Richard as your initiation."

Marie wore a new pair of shoes with no fur or tiger. *Unremarkable shoes inside her own house*, Junie thought.

"It's clever what you did, though," Clarisse drank from a large glass of pink wine, "saying Richard exposed himself in the parking lot. I never took you to be so diabolical."

"I just assumed he was like the others."

"Like who, dear?"

"You know. Men. Even when they used to notice me, it wasn't the greatest feeling."

Marie had a habit of addressing the group like she was in on a secret. "It's funny you see things that way. Have you always?"

"I think so?" Junie couldn't stop eating the candies once she gave into that first shiny silver disk. "Isn't that the way we all see things? I mean, my husband is decent. He has a good job, rarely yells, thinks I'm pretty enough I suppose. Half of the time he still pretends to see me when he comes home. I just assumed he's one of the good ones."

Marie aimed her words towards Junie. "Have you ever

asked yourself what about you is worth noticing, before you blame all the men?"

Another woman Junie didn't know opened a new bottle of wine. She sat her fit body too close to Marie on the couch so their bodies slithered together like fish. Their matching bags touched, the new possession Junie would covet all the way home.

The woman said, "What if they are all good and we are all bad?"

"Nobody on earth is all good or all bad."

There was no way the others knew that Marcus made them settle in the cul-de-sac after the hospital stay in hopes of keeping Junie's obsession with walking off into the night to a minimum. *It's literally a sack,* he had told her, *like a big bag you can't break out of.* But they would need groceries, and dry cleaning, and a possible pizza delivered on Friday nights like they used to before Marcus went around speaking to her like a child who acted bad without understanding exactly how.

"I like being bad." Maggs drank more wine.

"How are you supposed to sell real estate when you're always drunk?" Angela blended in with the furniture like she always did. "So, whose kitty is it this time?"

Junie had tired of this group the way she tired of every group she tried to infiltrate. Marcus still reminded her every night that they were stuck in the new house, with the new mortgage, whether or not things turned bad.

"It's my turn." Marie and her fishy friend giggled on the couch. They sat so close Junie thought they looked like a couple, hands and knees touching, so desirable they couldn't help desiring each other. "I want to sleep with one of your husbands. I don't care which one. I'll leave it up to you decide."

"How's that solidarity?" Junie asked, but no one responded. "The point of kitty parties is to help each other."

"Me getting to be with someone new after all these years will definitely help me. But you can leave Marcus out of this, if you don't think he's a worthy prize."

"Put his name in the mix, but I doubt any of this will be what you're expecting."

Into a top hat Marie retrieved from a hall closet, of course a woman like her would own a top hat, each woman wrote down her husband's name and tossed in the piece of paper. Marie moved the hat in a circular motion, as if an invisible liquid filled the bottom. She pulled out a name Junie didn't recognize, the husband of a woman on the fringe of the group who attended very few parties and stayed near the refreshment table. She smiled as Marie commented on the man, named Ken. Ken worked in the tallest building downtown. Ken had blue eyes and wore a lot of ties, worked out with Richard Somebody a few times a week. About ten years ago, he tried to market his own barbecue sauce.

Junie didn't want to be a part of the group anymore. She hoped Marcus would not accuse her of retreating into her dream self, as he called it. She really didn't want to spend money on ripe avocados or miniature pickles for the last months of her life before she vanished completely. "I don't think I'll be coming to any more of your parties. Thank you for having me, but it's obvious I don't fit in."

"You can't really mean that?" Marie sat up straight, almost like she had been mildly shocked. A light blue color spread across her face. Junie scanned the living room for a trick bulb.

"You can't leave. We need you." Maggs put her hand on Junie's shoulder. "You're the one we've been waiting for to complete our circle."

"Circle?"

"We thought for sure you'd figure it out by now. We're a coven."

"A coven?"

"Yes, we're witches."

Junie felt a chill zip up both arms. "I knew it. I knew you all acted closer than just neighbors, with that secret language of yours, and the way you never really eat, or get old. And I bet Marie isn't the only one with a lover, either."

"I'm definitely not." Marie removed her shoes. She nodded at the others, who stifled palpable laughter into varying blue shades of cocktail napkins. They also removed their shoes to leave a pile of heels on the white fur rug. "If only you would've thought to serve us eye of newt instead of all that cream cheese toast."

Junie said, "I remember reading something about hemlock, but I think it's poisonous. We also need a lizard's foot. If one of you knows where to get one, I'll prepare it at the next meeting however you like."

"What we really need is blood. And lots of it." Maggs now sat too close to Marie on the couch. She covered her mouth when she laughed. Her fingernails made four red slashes across her pale face.

That's why the fingernails, Junie thought, *and why Marcus always seems suspicious when I'm out past ten with any of them, even when I promise not to do anything weird.*

Junie ate more candy without registering any sensation but a dull throb behind her eyes from too much sugar. "Do you just get it from the butcher?"

"The blood needs to come from a human, ideally a male. If you don't mind hosting again so soon?" Marie placed one shoe back on only to dangle the thick heel off her foot. "Now who's going to tell Ken we're spending the night?"

From the foyer Junie still heard the cackle of the others. A shrill, impudent echo followed her down the front path towards her car when she decided to leave early. To collect her thoughts, she said. To get ready for next time.

That night she faced her sleeping husband in bed. This felt unusual, too intimate.

Her body always turned from him, edged so close to her side that each night she feared falling onto the rug. Junie watched Marcus dream. His eyes behind his lids darted back and forth. She knew wherever he had gone had nothing to do with her. The only sharp kitchen knife waited under her pillow as she tried to remember anatomy from the continuing education class she had taken years ago during a brief infatuation with figure drawing, an infatuation that ended abruptly the afternoon one of her favorite models caught Junie trying to follow him home.

Where can I stab so he will go quick but not hurt too much? Dear husband, sweet husband, sometimes, even though you forced me to move here after forcing me to go to the hospital after forcing me to stop taking random bus trips in the middle of the night without telling you first. At least you still pretend I'm alive.

Junie moved the knife, a small tool she watched Marcus use to pare apples, across his face to rest between his eyes.

Just one quick, quiet push, she thought. *One small cut for me, one giant cut for womankind.* But for some reason, nerves, obligation, a remembrance of the past love she once held for Marcus before things fell so far apart, she could not push the blade into his body. Not even a little superficial scratch to yield a speck of blood, the offering to the group she might collect on a napkin. A promise of solemn vows to come.

Was it too late to text Maggs? The housing market down and falling since CNN talked so much about China and Trump and tariffs gave Maggs no reason to rise early.

Junie reached out. "I can't do it," she texted. "I feel too weak. Or something."

"Can't do what?"

Junie imagined that click-clack sound of Maggs using her red nails to text back. Even imagining the sound caused a wave of nausea to quake through her body. "Stab my husband."

"Jesus, what r u talking about?"

Junie hated it when women her age responded to texts like teenagers. "Isn't it my turn to get blood for the group?"

"Junie we were only fucking with u. Which I hope u r doing 2 me now."

"Fucking with me about the blood?"

"The blood. The coven. Marie sleeping with Ken. ALL OF IT."

"Why would you do that? And I still don't even know who Ken is?" As Junie texted she gently removed the knife blade from between Marcus's temple, prayed he kept sleeping.

"We were just having fun. U r the first new woman in town in such a long time. But u take everything so literally. You're a hoot, girl. Now get some sleep and I'll call u tomorrow before I show the Hollyhock Lane house."

Junie dropped the knife onto her side of the rug, *be quiet, quiet,* and kicked the blade under the frame with a socked foot. She lay back on her pillow in the dark. Her phone bathed the room in an alien light. "But you told me that listing would never sell, and not to go for it, that it would be a waste of time?"

"Just effing with you again, Mama. Now get some Zzzz's. Coffee tomorrow, on me."

Junie felt more powerful not responding. She realized she would never again respond to Maggs, or anyone else in that circle, and possibly Marcus. Without moving the covers, without disturbing her own pillow, Junie left the bed the same way she slept in the bed as her husband snored himself into an immovable force.

She left her car in the lot, keys in the ignition. The bus station in this town was still new to her, but Junie made quick work of procuring a ticket as her feet pounded against the checkered floor in her Chinese knock-off slippers. Terminal, her one-way ticket, she thought to a town near a Canadian border, but never verified her final destination.

The bus ride felt the same as every other bus ride. The nocturnal American landscape passed as nothing but strings of headlights and taillights, stoplights and convenience stores. What was the point of ever being anywhere, really?

We were just fucking with you. All of us, we're only ever just fucking with you.

But I don't want to be fucked with anymore. The night caught inside the bus. Exhaust and over-traveled bodies thwarted any attempt at fresh air. The smell of the bus, usually a comfort in its predicted noxiousness, this time felt suffocating.

"I can't breathe." First Junie's protest sounded too quiet, a near whisper that she barely understood as coming from her own mouth. "I can't breathe," she said again, this time louder. The motion of the bus hit her with concentric circles of force as she stood. Her purse, the wallet with just enough mad money the others had mocked in that tone of collusion only middle-aged women can truly understand, rested on the seat next to her. Red taillights filled her view. Panic rose along the crest of each bump and jockey of the tires bearing down on the asphalt. "I need to get off the bus."

We could almost be flying, Junie thought. *A road paved in nothing but clouds. And all I have to do is jump.* She felt her way down the darkened bus towards a driver so silent, Junie wondered if the bus commandeered itself to that Canadian border town on autopilot.

"Please," she asked the driver, surprised to find an older woman behind the wheel, "I need to get off. I'm not feeling well. And I see you, which means I hope you see me."

"Can't let you off unless it's a sanctioned stop."

"But please. I think I might be sick. I need air. Can you make an exception, just this once?" Junie passed the boundary between the bus floor and the first step down to the double swinging door. "Please?" She banged against the door in the dark, one shoe lost on the stair tread like an urban Cinderella with no Prince Charming waiting for her on the other side. The smell of her armpits as she moved embarrassed her. "How about I just sneak off the next time you stop at a railroad track?"

Miles later, when tracks finally appeared, the driver reluctantly opening the door, Junie fled the bus into the night. She knew no one cared enough about an unknown woman to go after her. The man sitting closest to her empty seat and discarded purse took the cash from her wallet without checking for ID. He threw the purse back on what was once Junie's seat.

Walking down the railroad tracks in the middle of the night isn't half as scary as it sounds. Bugs kept Junie company. That insistent, ever-present hum, almost as if something either exciting, or deadly, waited for her around each new corner. From the blue-white arc on her flashlight phone, Junie saw the tracks go on and on. She stumbled a few times before memorizing the rhythm of walking between each railroad tie. She knew there was nothing left to do but follow the tracks. Maybe towards home, or maybe somewhere even worse.

As a teen, she had watched too many scary movies to hitchhike. If she got into a stranger's car, she knew she was never coming back. That was certain. And who would stop for her at this age? Who would even see her? Junie's thighs rubbed together as she loped on. A painful, prickly warmth grew as the cooling dawn air pushed her towards sunrise.

At a diner near the tracks, her first spotting of civilization, she realized with the impending daylight that her spontaneous bus journey had deposited her two states away from her new home. Junie got the attention of the waitress without having to ask. She looked to be a woman about the same age. *Much too old to be waiting on me*, she thought. Junie ordered a plate of eggs. When she pierced the golden yolks of two over-easy eggs with a bent fork tine, thick yellow egg gravy covered the bacon she left on her plate. After ordering more bacon, then adding the new pile of bacon to the first mound, Junie stared at the meat while the sun rose into late morning. She had forgotten to hide any money in any of her pockets before she fled the bus.

"You can't pay for that, can you?" the waitress asked after Junie turned down multiple offers for a coffee refill.

"Well," Junie stared into the woman's eyes, "normally I could, but I lost my purse on the bus, and then I lost my bus, and now I don't know where to catch another one, or where to go."

"Why don't I take my break and help you sort things out?"

"Why would you do that for me?"

"Let's just say someone helped me out once, a long time ago."

The waitress never told Junie her name, and did not wear a nametag. She liked not knowing the name of the woman who walked her out of the diner without the manager noticing. They stood close together in a back parking lot. The waitress offered Junie a cigarette.

"No thanks. I don't need another bad habit to get over."

"What are your current ones?" The waitress blew a gray cloud away from Junie's face. The cloud smelled like something dank burning from the inside out.

Junie's stomach grumbled. She regretted not eating her bacon.

"I follow home people I find interesting, usually without telling them. Sometimes I take buses to other towns in the middle of the night, without telling my husband. I've spent a lot of money ordering kitchen gadgets online, mostly vintage. I covet things I can't afford. I hate the women in my neighborhood. I obsess about being too plain. I can't accept that I'm disappearing."

"Why?"

"Because I used to be so vibrant. I felt so alive, once."

"When's the last time you felt like that, because I can't remember."

The cigarette vanished with a fast burn in the late morning. Heat undulated off the concrete surrounding the two women.

"In junior high. Basically before boys. I remember the happiest summer I spent lounging around the house, baking cake mixes for slumber parties, squeezing the leftover frosting between graham crackers."

"That sounds like heaven."

The smell of the dumpster wafted into Junie's nose. How could everything discarded from the restaurant immediately smell so rotten? Through a pierce of hunger she regretted eating anything there at all.

"I might not even be remembering things right."

"Why don't we have one tonight?"

"A slumber party?" All of Junie's nerves felt like they were burning from the inside out. But in a good way.

"A grown-up version. If you can throw a cake mix in a pan, I'll bring the wine."

"I'd love to," Junie backed away from the waitress, "but I'm pretty sure my husband has already reported me missing."

"I wish I could go missing sometimes. I doubt your husband is even looking for you yet." The waitress finished her cigarette. "I need to get back. Please just stay with me tonight? I've craved a proper girls' night for a really long time. No one around here is into it. I live right around the corner."

"Are you sure you're not afraid of me? Are you hitting on me?"

"I don't have anything worth stealing, and no, I'm not hitting on you." She extinguished her cigarette with her chunky black work shoe. "When you get back home, everyone will actually miss you. You won't be invisible anymore. It'll be the best feeling in the world. Even that bitch you mentioned with the fuzzy shoes will be happy you're okay."

The waitress handed Junie a jumble of keys on a ring and pointed her a block away. When Junie turned to wave goodbye, the waitress's outline rippled in the heat. Junie looked away before the waitress began to disappear.

From the waitress's apartment, Junie saw the diner roof. Exhaust coming from a large pipe smelled like French fries when she leaned closer. So many unknown objects surrounded her as she waited for the waitress to come home.

What a funny sentence, she thought, *waiting for the waitress*.

The waitress owned a small yellow fridge humming next to a banana-yellow counter. A scan of the cupboards revealed a woman who preferred those chocolate-marsh-mallow-coated low-fat cookies over the better-tasting, fatty kind. And bagged popcorn, canned soup, the brand of cheese in the bright yellow box you don't have to refrigerate, but no boxes of cake mix. Junie couldn't even throw something together with a few of those blue mini-boxes of muffin mix.

The waitress held her work schedule to the fridge with a little magnet shaped like an avocado. Each day said the same hours, the breakfast and lunch shifts, the name "Junie" written above the schedule in handwriting Junie recognized as her own. She looked down at her body. A light blue apron secured itself around the dark blue diner uniform the waitress wore that morning.

"Where are you?" Junie said to the bare living room.

Nothing registered a sense of the familiar, except a small porcelain bowl, nicked around the edge and filled with yellow M&Ms. In the bedroom, Junie found a small, tidy bed. A flowered yellow lamp matched the flowered yellow spread. In the bedroom closet a row of waitress uniforms waited to be pressed. The bottom sat empty, except for one fake Gucci tiger slipper lined in unknown fur.

In the spare bedroom, Junie found a pile of old missing person flyers with torn edges. She recognized her own phony smile peering out of the pixelated black and white. Junie sat at the kitchen table. She lit and smoked a cigarette before remembering she was a non-smoker. When was the waitress coming back? Should she make dinner? What about the slumber party? What about the cake? A scan of the empty fridge prompted Junie to go looking.

"What are you doing back here already?" a man who must've been the manager asked Junie when she stood at the front door. She stared down at her ill-fitting work shoes.

"What do you mean, back here already? And do you swear you can really see me?" Junie held out her arm towards the man. He did not try to swat her hand away.

"I can see that you aren't doing your side work."

"I'm happy to do side work, thrilled, actually, if you tell me what that means."

An older woman wearing the same blue uniform pointed in Junie's direction. "Hey, you need to go home so you'll be ready for the kitty party tonight. You promised to show everyone how they work. Don't make me sorry I covered your shift."

"Yes, of course. I guess I forgot."

"Forgot?"

"Excuse me? Kate?" Junie found the woman's nametag over her right breast. The tag sat a little crooked. Sauce smeared one corner. "How long have I worked here?"

"At least a few months, maybe longer? You just appeared one day with a uniform. We've never asked where you got it, or what happened to Alice. Or maybe her name was Lisa? Am I still bringing the square eggs tonight? Thanks again for lending me your cuber. My husband loves it."

Back at the apartment, Junie remembered how to make pudding in a cloud without much effort. Having never developed a taste for whipped topping, she guessed the women coming over later didn't know the difference between real and artificial, anyway.

And they'll probably ask for money in their kitty, nothing exciting like we did back in the day.

She covered the side counter with a yellow placemat and arranged six puddings in clouds. On a small yellow plate she unwrapped and stacked slices of American cheese. To the cheese, Junie added a handful of peanuts, would pretend she found the recipe in a vintage cookbook if anyone asked, would pretend she forgot about redecorating the apartment in so much yellow after throwing all the other waitress's belongings in the town landfill earlier that summer, even the large flatscreen and a stack of what looked like interesting books.

"This doesn't feel right," Junie spoke to her yellow kitchen. "I'm not really supposed to be here. Marcus must be worried sick."

Not one to cancel any party, Junie let the women into the apartment as they began to show up after their diner shifts. Most she sort of recognized as coworkers who had shown her the ropes, the kitchen slang, the way to count tips and how to pin her nametag on her uniform as straight as possible.

"Please help yourself to everything." Junie pointed to the puddings, the cheese plate, the bottles of soda cooling on the counter in a metal bucket filled with ice. "I need to check on one more thing."

Her feet ached, she guessed from a diner shift she remembered in traces of images and noise. She stood outside the apartment. Junie dialed Marcus's number on her cell phone. After all those months of pretending to be missing, her heart pummeled her ribs while she waited to hear his voice.

"You need to quit calling this number," Marcus said without a hello first.

"Marcus?"

"Yes, and we've gone over the same thing night after night for weeks. When will you get it through your mind that I don't want anything to do with whoever you are."

"But it's Junie."

"Is this your angle, taking advantage of a man with a missing wife?"

"I'm sorry I ever went missing. If I had any idea how screwed up I was, I would've asked you to help me again."

"Here." Marcus spoke to a disembodied female voice that Junie imagined to be sitting on her pink couch in their living room. "Maybe you can let this woman know how serious I am? One more call and I swear I'll get the police involved."

Junie recognized the impatient breath of the woman on Marcus's phone. "Maggs? What are you doing with my husband?"

"How do you know my name? How did you get this number?"

"It's me, Junie."

One of the other women yelled out the front door of the apartment if they could start the kitty party without her. Junie yelled back yes. She felt her apron tighten around her middle.

"Marcus, she says it's Junie. A strange woman has Junie's phone. This could be the lead we've been looking for."

"I did not steal my own goddamn phone, Maggs. Why are you doing this to me?"

"Where are you, miss, and why do you have Junie's phone? Miss, miss?"

From the courtyard Junie heard the women laughing as if a male stripper had crashed their over-the-hill hen party. Once in a while, silence spread through the gathering as she paced in front of the door. A chorus of spoons clinked against the sides of the dessert glasses.

"It would be so much better for me just to stay here," Junie spoke to the apartment door's peephole, "but this is not where I belong."

It sounded like much more cocktail than search party, those voices behind the door Junie put names to in a blink. Maggs, Marie, Angela, Clarisse, that one woman whose body always glided through rooms like a slimy little fish. The front door refused to budge as her fingers fiddled with the knob. *What a defeat*, she thought, *to ring the bell outside my own house.*

"You must be here for the search party." Marie left Junie standing on her own front porch as she yelled to the others, "And you all laughed when I posted our meetings on Instagram."

Marie led Junie past her own pink couch to a row of card tables arranged in the living room. Flyers with Junie's face covered most of the tables. A woman Junie didn't recognize scribbled in a notebook at one table.

"What's she doing?" Junie hoped no one had cooked in her kitchen. The rugs needed a good vacuuming.

"She's the psychic Marie brought in."

The woman held a ballpoint pen between her fingers like a blue cigarette. She rotated through a series of what came across as choreographed gestures. Pen to mouth to lightly chew on the cap, pen held away from her lips, as if the writing instrument really was something she could smoke. Pen on notebook paper, the psychic's hand moving in erratic swirls. Her eyes stayed closed.

"How could Marcus believe in this? He's been an atheist since college."

"Girls!" Marie shouted towards the tables. "We have the first Junie Springs scholar in our midst." She stared at Junie. "Marcus's religion is not listed on Junie's Wikipedia page. However you're getting your info, and I trust it's accurate, you must be digging deep." Marie patted Junie's back. Her hand recoiled at the dampness of her uniform.

"I've been in a hurry and forgot to change out of my work clothes."

"I assumed you were acting out some sort of Junie cosplay. They've been popping up on YouTube more and more. It's probably because of the *Dateline* exposure. I don't care how old Keith Morrison is, he's a fox." Marie scrutinized the waitress uniform. She smiled at the nametag, JUNIE in sharpie pen on light pink plastic. "You look great, but uncomfortable. Why don't you take off your shoes and relax?"

The Gucci tiger slippers wrapped tight around Marie's feet. "Aren't they fun? Would you like to wear them awhile, *Junie?*" She chortled as she pointed to the nametag. "I like you already."

"Why are you pretending that I'm not me? I know you can fucking see me."

"Please, no swearing in front of the psychic. Would you like to meet Marcus? He's with the police. The poor man goes every Wednesday and Friday afternoon to discuss any leads." Angela folded a flyer. She placed the flyer in an envelope to add to a large stack crowded into a cardboard box. "I'd sure love to get my hands on him. His devotion to his missing wife really turns me on."

"Me too."

"Yeah, me too."

With her finger Junie outlined her profile on a flyer. "This isn't a very good picture of her."

"So you knew her, like in real life?" Maggs stared at Junie without dropping eye contact.

"I thought I did, once, but I guess I was wrong. She just seemed to disappear, before my very eyes. I did go to one or two of her kitty parties, way back."

Marie studied the waitress uniform. "I thought you looked familiar. Do you live around here?"

"I live pretty close."

"Then maybe you could check on Marcus every now and then, at your convenience? We all worry about him."

The other women packed up their things without looking at her. Junie only recalled engaging with half the ladies who buzzed around the card tables like large, well-dressed insects.

"I'd love to."

She watched as the others checked the time on their phones. They gave up shoving flyers into envelopes for another day. Marie told the group it was her turn to cook for Marcus, but Junie volunteered.

"I'm a pretty good cook, plus I've learned a lot at the diner," she said while the group showed itself out her front door without much protest.

"He doesn't like green beans. At all." Clarisse stopped at the front door. Her serious tone made Marcus matter more to Junie then than during their entire marriage.

Angela opened her purse. "And here's a list of things he absolutely won't talk about. No politics at the table, even though CNN is going to run a story on Junie in the coming weeks."

"Are you serious?" Junie took the list of Marcus's least favorite foods. "What makes her so newsworthy?"

Marie said, "The fact that she is one hundred percent ordinary. Nothing about her is special. Her looks are plain, some might even say ugly. Her thoughts, the way she talks, the way she cooks. All ordinary. Even the way she fucks, as Marcus let slip weeks ago on one of those really long nights. We had canvassed the neighborhood, drank way too much after. And be prepared for the knocking. It'll start soon."

"Marcus doesn't like hot sauce either," Junie said, but the group all got into their cars without acknowledging her. She hollered towards their taillights, "Who will be knocking?"

Heat fried the zucchini into soft, brown coins while asparagus let off its nutty green aroma in another pan. Junie thawed chicken breasts on the counter for a quick stir-fry. She tried to guess when her husband would be back from looking for the version of his wife she knew had never existed. The doorbell rang. Two teen girls stared at her from the front porch when she answered. They wore black T-shirts with Junie's face silkscreened in white. The girls ignored the way Junie's face matched the face on the shirts.

"Is there anything of hers we could have? Please?"

The smell of zucchini going from caramelized to burnt escaped past the girls into the night.

"Why would you want something from someone you don't know? And why do you think we'd give you anything, even if we had it to give?"

"Come on, I told you this was stupid," one girl said to the other.

Junie saw an outie navel beneath one of the tight T-shirts. Junie's silkscreened mouth curved and distorted over the hidden, hard flesh button. She wanted to poke her finger into the girl's stomach until she reached the other side.

"You won't get it, since you're so old, and normal, but Junie is our hero."

"I need to check dinner now. Marcus doesn't enjoy burnt food."

Junie shut the screen. The girls popped the screen latch with little effort, leaned against the molding. Next time, she would sauté her asparagus tips in butter. *No more olive oil. I wasn't thinking. I know better.* The front door sprang towards her face with the weight of the girls against the knob. Panic spread through her body. Her heart thudded in a strange spot right in the middle of her throat. *These girls are too young to understand much of anything.*

"She's our hero because she ran away."

"Yeah," the prettier of the two licked her lip gloss. "None of us think she was abducted. She hated her stupid life and decided to do something about it. We'd kill to be able to do that."

"But you have your whole lives ahead of you, and how do you know nothing bad happened to her?"

The girls laughed. One of them pointed to the large, mannish silkscreened jawline. "Because she's nobody special."

"Who would abduct her?" the other said.

"If she's nobody special, how come you two are even here?"

"We saw online she's the new thing to be into, so we're into her now, too."

Junie examined the girls under the porch light. "You know, you both take after her a little around the eyes."

"We do? Do you really mean it?"

The girls hugged each other.

"You wouldn't just tell us that, right? You must've known her?"

One girl elbowed her friend. "What the hell, Mason? Know, not known. Junie is out there, and someday she'll come back to this town and tell all of us what it's like to make it through to the other side."

"To the other side of what?" Junie asked.

"To the other side of something more exciting than here."

One of them handed Junie an extra shirt from her bag. "This will be a little tight but still might fit you. Check out the local news on your laptop. You can follow Junie updates on the home screen."

She sent the girls away with a handful of flyers.

Junie remembered Marcus's password. She opened his laptop and typed in the local news channel's website. To the left of the news alerts flashed a red box with a white center. Junie Springs, missing 120 days. Beneath the red box she clicked a link to YouTube videos. In the videos, both young girls and grown women peddled what they called "Junie merch." It sounded like almost every female within a few-hundred-mile radius of Junie's home adorned herself in Junie T-shirts, carried Junie backpacks.

They shunned makeup after learning she didn't wear any. Some girls posted lengthy videos on how to apply makeup to look like you weren't really wearing it. On eBay, Junie saw four vintage egg cubers listed as her authentic cuber. Under the sink she found her cuber sitting in the old tattered box where she left it. Recipes popped up on other sites for cream cheese toast, and her

peanut-topped American cheese. Pink lemonade dominated another blog. Women she had never met wrote
about how they used to drink pink lemonade on the pink
couch in Junie's living room. Plus the recipe was wrong.
She never once added raspberries to her drink for color.
Like most things in life, real pink lemonade isn't even
really that pink, just like real missing women are very
different from the creatures the headlines try turning them
into.

The doorbell rang. Junie left the chicken cooking.
Lower sodium soy sauce for Marcus, as per the list. One
of the girls who stood before her moments earlier handed
Junie a plastic object.

"We forgot to give you a mask. If you put it on, you'll
look exactly like her."

Junie carried the mask into the kitchen, the chicken
almost burning in its pan. When she held the plastic mask
against her face, it filled her with nostalgia for a past she
had never expected to miss on all those secret bus rides
into the night. Plastic nose in the shape of her nose
clinging to her own nose. Every feature on her face
followed.

In the hall bathroom mirror, the mask became her real
face, its stiff form making a popping sound, almost like a
fire, whenever Junie moved. Slowly, she began to teach
herself to ignore the imposter who waited beneath. Maybe
Marcus would learn to ignore the sound, the overwhelm-

ing plastic smell, in exchange for living with the woman the world, in only a few quick months, had trained him to miss? She assumed her husband had reached the point in his grief where he would believe almost anything. The mask would turn her into the version of Junie he had always secretly wanted, the version that would never follow another man home, or get on a bus; the version of Junie that would never grow old, because the mask would never age. She would never have to fear vanishing again.

The mask began to fit itself onto Junie's face like a second, slightly ominous skin. Something about the eyes never quite matched up as she pushed the stir fry around in its pan. Moving one way caused the left eye hole of the mask to press on her lashes until one side of her face froze in a slow, permanent wink. Sweat formed between her cheeks and the cheeks of the mask. She itched. Swallowing began to sound labored when Junie pursed her lips against the pink-lipped mask. Junie plated the chicken stir fry close to the time Marcus usually came home from work.

Marcus's favorite wine waited next to the plate. Junie sat wearing the mask of her face, head bent in what looked like prayer. Tomorrow, she would call one of those computer tech guys to show her how to place the Junie Springs missing days counter on her homepage. A few Etsy shops might cut deals with her on merchandise, if she proved a provenance of having once known the real Junie. Cheese fondue felt appropriate for the coming kitty party, where she hoped each woman would come wearing a mask of Junie's face, too.

The air around the dining table nearly cracked from her building excitement to meet Marcus for the first time, as the person she finally wanted to be.

LIKE

Shelby arranged her neon pink platter of mini-mini cupcakes next to Fiona's mini cupcakes. The two girls, at twenty-seven both technically women, bumped their flowered, Bohemian party dresses into each other to get the best photo of their birthday offerings. Cell phones battled at the ends of their glittery fingernails for the best spot to snap a shot of the décor.

Fiona examined the cupcakes by pushing the zoom button on her phone screen. "OMG! I can't believe you found cupcakes even smaller than mine. And how did they silkscreen an entire sugar unicorn on top of each one?"

Shelby snapped more pictures. The candid, sometimes blurry, shots she uploaded to Facebook, Instagram, Twitter, Snapchat, and to her cupcake album on Pinterest. She scanned her Facebook wall. "I already have 43 likes!"

"Make that 44!" Clarissa shouted from the other end of the private room, in the back of a fancy salad restaurant, where the group had decided to celebrate Naomi turning twenty-eight.

Quinn carried a tower of regular-sized cupcakes topped with mini cupcakes then topped with mini-mini cupcakes though, being a transplant from the nearest big city, she called them bite-sized. "Don't they look French?"

"I'm liking them on your page right now," Clarissa said. To the party she brought gift bags filled with fake moustache finger tattoos, bandages shaped like vegan bacon, and crazy cat lady erasers.

"These are so cool!" Fiona shoved her phone inside one of the bags to take a photo. "23 likes in 12 seconds. That must be a new record," she said to Quinn.

Quinn, the girl from the city who wore mismatched prints and oversized sweaters a year before they became a trend, used her phone to scroll Instagram. "For me not really."

"Shh, everyone. Naomi is on the way."

The girls hid behind varying heights of cupcakes. They yelled, "Surprise!" when Naomi walked into the party room. Each found it hard to take her own picture, Naomi's picture, a group picture and a picture of the mini-mini (bite-sized) cupcakes simultaneously, yet none of the girls let on. So many photos were posted and tweeted and Instagrammed in the first three minutes of the party, none of the girls were sure whose photos to "like" first.

"I think we should click 'like' on Shelby's page because

she brought the unicorn cupcakes."

"No, definitely Quinn because of the tower."

"What about Naomi? It's her party so we better post on her page first."

Naomi had already photographed herself next to the cupcake tower, then popping an entire mini cupcake into her mouth followed by holding up her left index finger, decorated with one of the moustache tattoos. A vegan bacon bandage wrapped her middle finger.

"How did she do all of that so fast?" Clarissa asked. "And look, she already has 217 likes!"

Quinn stared at her own phone. Out of Naomi's earshot she said, "If she has so many 'friends' then how come I'm the only one who brought a cupcake tower, with edible glitter that I sprinkled on myself?"

Shelby smoothed the wrinkles in her party dress. She and the others clustered around the table like pink moths drawn to the siren call of piped frosting. "Why don't you post an Instagram story about the edible glitter and see who responds first?"

Some of the others held gift bags close to their faces for expertly posed selfies. No one tasted a cupcake, no matter the size, unless someone was right there to capture the spontaneously posed moment. (There was never a real worry that another girl would not be phone-ready at all times.)

After the first round of cupcake fawning and dress

complimenting, complete with photos and comparisons of fabrics, the group decided to read their Instagram comments.

"Should we clear away the presents?" someone asked.

"Naomi's already opened them all. Look, she's wearing the scarf I embroidered for her."

"The one with the butterfly wearing a suit and tie?"

"No, the other one, with the smiling geranium feeding a cupcake to a butterfly wearing a suit and tie."

Clarissa rubbed her fake tattoo onto her index finger. As she took a photo of her finger under her nose she said to Quinn, "I think she should've waited until we all sat down and opened each gift separately after reading the card out loud that came with each present. I didn't spend an hour on a D-I-Y blog studying gift wrap for no reason."

Shelby, Clarissa, Quinn, Fiona, and Naomi, who the group called Edamame whenever they all went for sushi, but in a way that could only ever be interpreted, tone-wise, as Naomi most definitely being in on the joke, each stared at her newest photo of the cupcake tower, then at the actual cupcake tower until, in a simultaneous blue flash followed by an all-consuming darkness as they huddled around the table in the back of the fancy salad restaurant, each phone turned itself off at the same moment.

It took longer than any of the girls would guess to stop staring at their blank phones, stop pressing the on buttons, stop swiping their fingernails across the unresponsive screens.

Quinn said, with an edge of panic etched behind her voice, "We must be in one of those places that blocks reception at a certain time each night when it gets close to dinner."

Shelby pushed her "on" button over and over with a glittery pink French tip. "Is it legal to do that because, seriously, right now I feel totally violated."

"I think I'm right, though." Quinn from the nearest big city knew how to ride public transportation. She also assumed a knowledge of various electronic devices; when they worked, why service was dropped and the legality of such an act. "You know, like how they tell you to turn everything off when you get on a plane?"

Fiona scanned the party room. "I thought that was because of terrorism?"

"This feels like terrorism to me," Clarissa said.

Naomi, who still wore both embroidered scarves, one looped strategically on top of the other to show both patterns, said, "When I turned twenty-five my parents offered to send me to Paris for a month. I said no way once I found out they couldn't guarantee cell service over there. And their social media is, like, European."

"They call them mobiles over there, not cells," Quinn said.

"I heard their television is broadcast in European, too. And they, like, never eat cupcakes." Fiona kept her finger, another one with a faux moustache tattoo, firm against her phone's "on" button.

"This is ridiculous," Quinn said after multiple dead screen swipes. "I'm getting the manager."

In the front dining area of the fancy salad restaurant no one added chopped chicken to their salad bowls or scooped cottage cheese on their plates for dessert. The patrons sat with phones clutched in their hands. They, too, stared into blackness. Children too young to have anyone to text looped the salad bar's perimeter or watched croutons settle atop the viscous dressings. Some ate sunflower seeds by the handful while others dumped buckets of shredded radish and cucumber, even at a young age deemed the least deserving of the fancy salad offerings, onto the ground near their expressionless parents.

"It's bad. Really, really bad," Quinn said back in the party room as she shut the doors behind her. "It's a nightmare out there."

"Have we been blocked?" Shelby asked.

Fiona said, "Is it on purpose? If so I want my fourth of the room rental deposit back."

"What monster would make a birthday party a no-cell zone? What a total fascist." (Shelby had recently seen the movie about the soldiers who tried to locate all those stolen paintings in World War II.)

"It's worse than no service in just this room, or even this restaurant. Look outside." Quinn pointed to the window centered above the party table.

None of the others thought to look outside because they never really looked, or ventured, too far from their phones. In a rustle of large hats and embroidered dresses the girls rushed to the window, each still gripping a phone in one hand, dead or not. Well, they didn't really rush since, on the off-chance someone, somewhere, had a phone that still worked, they wanted to look good just in case they were caught in the middle of their trauma. From the window they could see how, up and down the avenue, people stared at their phones. A few teenage girls sobbed while others pretended to comfort the sobbing. Tendons on both sides of businessmen's necks flexed to a sharp, disturbing tautness. Mothers who didn't know which house their children played at panicked as they hit their phones over and over in what looked like pitiful attempts to perform a sort of electronic CPR.

"Has a bomb dropped?" Shelby asked towards the window.

"Do they really not eat cupcakes in Paris?" Fiona asked no one in particular.

Quinn stepped away from the window. "It's more like all the world's phones just quit working at the same time. Maybe it's a satellite thing, or maybe it's just one of those things?"

Girls like Quinn, with their purposefully mismatched socks and their overly long Zooey Deschanel bangs, also thought it sounded cool when they quoted lyrics from the Great American Songbook.

Shelby had had just about enough of that type of girl. She was sick of the uncountable times she'd felt forced to "like" Quinn's Facebook photos of vintage roller skates and paint-your-own pottery gnomes. "Just one of those things?" she repeated in the form of a question. "How can you say something like that?" She undid the top button on her dress. "Does anyone else think it's too hot in here?"

She turned to see Clarissa, her dress sleeves rolled up to reveal her J.D. Salinger-quote-tattooed inner arms, sitting in front of the cupcake tower. Instead of pulling a bite-sized, edible-glittered cupcake off one of the larger cupcakes, the smallest morsel of pastry the only acceptable size to eat without having to defend her reckless dietary decisions to a very thin jury of her peers, Clarissa held her phone as if it was a hammer. She whacked a giant cupcake, plus its mini and mini-mini top, into several frosting-sticky pieces.

"What are you doing?" Fiona pulled Clarissa's phone out of the mess.

"Don't you see how nothing has any meaning if you can't post it online? What's the point of liking real-life things if they can't then be 'liked' in the virtual world?"

"She's right." Naomi pulled her scarves tighter around her neck. "What's the point of seeing something beautiful if we can't post it?"

Fiona teetered back in her wedge sandals. "Because it is life and we get to live it, that's why!"

"Life?" Naomi said. "Isn't that just something we do, or a series of somethings we all do, to have a more interesting Instagram?"

Shelby stood near the mini-mini sugared unicorn cupcakes. "What's the point of eating something so cute if I can't take a selfie while I eat it, then post it online so everyone else can tell me how cute they think it is, too?" She balled her hands and punched her mini-mini cupcake platter until nothing but a pink glittering mass remained.

"We all just need to calm down," either Clarissa or Fiona said. The girls were all blending into one embroidered dress of panic. "This can't last forever. There's no way the world, or even this town, has stopped cell service permanently. That can't happen, can it? Wait, what are you doing? Knock it off!"

Naomi had removed her top scarf while Shelby obliterated the cupcakes. She wrapped the embroidered silk around Fiona's neck as Fiona droned on and on about the importance of life before social media. After tying the scarf in a bow, Naomi kept pulling. The group watched Naomi strangle the air out of Fiona until her face, and her lips and even her fingertips where she had clawed to break free, turned blue. Her body slid to the floor.

"Now that's the color that actually suits her," Naomi said. "Wish I could post a picture."

With cupcaked hands waving the air in front of her Shelby whined, "Why did you do that?"

"Yeah, why *did* you do that?" Quinn, who in the big city had seen her share of strangulations, or at least heard about them on the news, asked in a calm voice.

"Because I wanted to feel something, and I hate her for taking that away from me. She is responsible for ruining my party and everyone knows it."

Quinn asked, "You think she ruined your party by calling those stupid things she brought mini-mini cupcakes?"

Naomi straightened her dress, rolled down her belled sleeves. "I blame her for everything, but I guess I don't really know why."

"The way she was droning on and on about real life being just as important as the social media universe was really starting to piss me off, too. And those mini-mini cupcakes are pretty lame, though I just remembered Shelby brought the mini-minis, not Fiona," Clarissa said.

"I don't even know which one is which," Naomi answered.

"Funny," Quinn said, "I never have, either. I mean, of course they're all my BFFs but, you know, who isn't?"

The group agreed not to talk about the things they missed the most, the collective wisdom of their social media pages drying up in their memories like something perishable exposed to heat.

"You know, killing her wasn't nearly as much fun as I'd always imagined it would be, what with no one else knowing about it except all of you. Our small group as witnesses didn't feel world-wide-web enough to me." Naomi pulled her other embroidered scarf too tight around her own neck.

Quinn stood close enough to pull one scarf end while Shelby stepped over Fiona's still body to reach for the other end of Naomi's scarf. "Is this doing anything for you?" she asked Shelby over Naomi's seizing form.

The more Naomi struggled to break free of the scarf, the more she convulsed before falling to the ground in an embroidered pile. Off went her big brown hat.

"Not like I thought it would," Shelby said over Naomi's body crumpled at her feet. "It feels about the same as the cupcakes, really."

"Do you want to divide up her presents when we're done?"

"And the gift bags?" In the party room corner Clarissa pretended to pose for selfies with her defunct camera phone. "Am I getting the bags in the pictures?" she asked to no one standing near the far wall.

"Wait a minute. We have to get a hold of ourselves." Shelby stepped over the bodies of both Fiona and Naomi. She grabbed Clarissa's phone. "We aren't thinking straight."

"Yeah," Quinn said. "We need to put these pics on

both Facebook and Instagram at the same time." She swiped her cotton candy French tips across her dead screen. "See?" She, too, addressed the far party room wall.

"Wow!" the two girls said in unison. "You're right."

"I wonder if we should order our salads now?" Shelby, without Fiona and her skinny legs wobbling around on those strangely hypnotic ankle boots and Naomi's long waist, made to look even longer in a Venice Beach sheath as it caved in on itself like one of the Olsen twins, stuffed several mini-mini cupcakes, squashed and now imperfect, into her mouth. "I mean, we already paid for five all-you-can-eat plates as part of the rental." She scooped up fluffy mounds and shoved her frosting-heavy fingers deep into her mouth. "And even though we can't take any pictures of the salad bar, I am still pretty hungry."

"I planned on documenting each salad bar item along with a quippy comment. I already thought a bunch of them out. Wait, I'll be right back." Clarissa left Quinn and Shelby in the party room, surrounded by torn gift wrap, crumbled cupcakes, shattered sugar unicorns. She stepped over gift bags that spilled their bacon-shaped bandages and crazy cat lady erasers across the room's tiled floor. She heard the sound of broken acrylic nails as she smashed her ballet flats over one of Naomi's cold, stiffening hands.

"Tell me what it's like living in a city," Shelby asked Quinn with a mouth dyed pink from frosting.

Quinn spent several minutes not speaking. She sat next to Shelby and her cupcake pile. What did it feel like living in a city? A search of her most recent memories revealed the blue-grey light of her phone screen, the pervasive black rectangle held at arm's length in front of any street scene, food cart, art gallery, subway ride. This black rectangle became a blind spot blocking every vision. The bowl of pho at that one place with the spring rolls: in her catalog of memories the bowl became her mind's eye staring through her phone at a picture of a bowl. Her favorite museum's traveling Francis Bacon triptych of Lucien Freud: a blurry yellow Instagram photo, the painting's dimensions turned from three rectangles to one fat, computer-retro-tinted square. Her cat equaled pictures on Facebook of her cat. Her boyfriend equaled Pinterest subcategories for boys with beards, boys dressed as lumberjacks, boys holding cans of Pabst Blue Ribbon.

While Shelby ran her sticky hands through the frosting mess to reveal more cupcake underbelly, Quinn said, "It's funny to realize that no one's ever asked me in person how I feel about anything."

"In person?" Shelby said. With slick pinked fingers she peeled back the wrappers on a few remaining cupcakes.

Quinn moved close enough to Shelby to reach out and touch part of a cupcake. She decided not to reach. "Well of course my friends always comment on my social media, but they never comment IRL."

"I'm asking you so I can comment for real."

Another city-life-flashing-before-Quinn's-eyes moment only revealed her obvious truth. "Living in a city feels no different than living here. It's all just comments and likes."

Clarissa came back to the party room with two plates piled in salad bar offerings. "Okay, girls." She set the plates at the head of the table after brushing Naomi's leftover wrapping paper onto the floor. The paper fell in slow folds to cover Fiona's face like a shroud.

On the cleared table Clarissa stacked the food into a line of tiny, colorful pyramids. "See," she pointed first to the peas, "if I was on Facebook I would take a picture now." She pretended to hold an invisible phone close to the green tower. "And I'd caption it Only Peas for Meez, Please."

Shelby laughed in the middle of cupcake bites. She said, "That's a good one."

Next to the pile of pickled beets Clarissa pointed and said, "Beat It! Get it? Beet spelled with an 'e' and an 'a' like that old Michael Jackson song."

She pointed to more piles: "Even Yeezus Likes Cottage Chee-zus."

"And We Can't Stop (Eating Kidney Beans)."

"Olive U."

Quinn stood. She moved away from the salad bar pyramids on bright display. "I think we get the point."

Shelby kept laughing and eating, eating and laughing,

pulling wrapper after crumb-coated wrapper off cupcakes both large and small. "Yeezus likes Cottage Chee-zus. That one kills!"

And then the laughing stopped.

"I'm glad you think so, Shelby. Wait, Shelby?"

In the middle of the party room Shelby stood from the table. She clutched both hands to her throat.

"Oh my God, she's choking!" Quinn rushed towards Shelby's reddening face.

"Hurry, hurry!" Clarissa said as Quinn wrapped her arms around Shelby and began to perform the Heimlich maneuver.

"Wait, did you hear that? My phone beeped! It's working again! It's working! Look! Look!"

Quinn dropped Shelby, a mound of cupcake still lodged in her throat, and raced for her phone. "I can't see it with all this wrapping paper in the way."

"And the bodies," Clarissa said. She snapped a photo of Fiona and Naomi. "Look, it worked! I already have three likes in less than a minute."

"Think you can take a picture of me giving the Heimlich to Shelbs?" Quinn straightened her dress. In no hurry, she fixed her hair in her phone screen after hitting the reverse camera button. She tried to pick up Shelby.

"Like, totally."

Shelby collapsed on the floor, her slight weight too heavy for Quinn to steady as her body shut down without air. Quinn leaned toward Shelby's body. "Well, at least get a photo of me looking sad near her, okay?"

"Already pinned it!" Clarissa said with a tone of glee that resonated around the party room. "I'll move to Fiona and Naomi next."

"Yeah, totally." Quinn placed a small cupcake next to the bodies of Shelby, Fiona and Naomi. "I wish we had a flower for each of them, or a vegan bacon Band-aid or something."

SERVICE PROVIDER

The black van pulled away from the white house with the red trim the night Elaine and Terry sat on their front porch sharing a bottle of wine.

"New neighbor?" Terry said.

"I'm almost positive I saw the same van a few days ago when I was jogging. Parked in front of the house of those people we used to know."

"What people?"

"We used to know them but I can't remember how." Elaine motioned to her wine. What ease, after so many married years, pretending to enjoy Terry's nightly imbibe. She hated the taste, even the jam-sweet dessert Sauternes. Yes, Elaine loathed the taste, the smell, the inevitable morning blur, but she never complained about the shared wine dulling the recollections of all those people, places, interstices of time not worth remembering.

Terry poured her another glass. "I definitely think it was the new neighbor."

The new neighbor had moved into the other house the couple considered buying on nights when the wine flowed like the description on the label promised. Terry loved words like "investment property" almost as much as Elaine loved to imagine fielding future Vrbo reservations. She wanted the new neighbor's house, red trim against white paint like a deep, dark cut, to be her escape for the next few months. Each time she drove by the for-sale sign, Elaine imagined changing the red trim to white, the white house to yellow. The hanging baskets needed to go, too, left on each side of the stone front steps by the previous owners. Such sad, wilted petunias, made sadder during her evening walks when the sun blued the yard and the flowers shut up tight. The porch meant to be her porch called for baskets of bright, hearty fuchsias, their languid tumble of flowers slightly sexual in the afternoon heat.

On those wine-flowing, jammy-sweet nights, as much as Terry pretended to want the same thing, he found his way out of every slightly drunken daydream.

"The steps need work."

"You said you know a guy who can fix steps? The one who owes your brother a favor?"

"I don't like the trim."

"That's why a few weeks ago you agreed to paint it white."

"Does white even go over red?"

"It's not like when you paint something red it can never

be another color."

"It's not?"

Terry picked at a hunk of salmon lodged in a back tooth. These days it was all salmon and kale, morning workouts and afternoon jogs to stave off growing older. Elaine hated salmon.

"You told me you know a guy who can cover over any color."

"I don't remember saying that."

"But you did, hon. Look, it's another black van, or the same black van. Look."

Terry never looked.

The new neighbor moved in the day Elaine decided to stop noticing new neighbors. Terry accused her of watching them like one of those women from an old sitcom. A nosy neighbor whose concerned brows crank up the canned laughter a little too loud. *Plus the audience is always in on the joke*, she thought, *and leaves the neighbor out.*

But I'm never out, Terry, husband with a name I have grown to hate over ten years of saying it, mostly when you're at work and I find another wet towel on the bathroom floor. Always when you roll me on my side, every other weekend or so, the way women in movies want morning sex. Real women crave sleep and pancakes, Terry. Wake up.

How I hate you as I face the bedroom curtain I

sometimes leave open. Maybe one of the neighbors will walk by when you're finishing, all grunt and no apology, and see me, the woman who lives inside a cage no different from the cage they will stroll back into after their weekend constitutional. I'm not even worth the price of admission.

Maybe one of the neighbors will walk by, but not the new neighbor.

This new neighbor had stolen her house. Elaine didn't want, or need, it, but craved fixing the house up. Working from home—she sold vintage pottery online to buyers with specific tastes and the kind of discretionary income that funds everything from bake sales to domestic terrorism—made Elaine crave some place she officially needed to be besides in front of a laptop poring over another auction house catalog. A place she could decorate the exact way she decorated her home, that mastered tone of suburban inoffensiveness replete with vintage vases. Perhaps an ivy-covered pergola out back? A Little Free Library on a post out front?

Look, she imagined bragging to Terry on an evening walk-by. *Look, I just finished the trim. Spring Crème. How could it be any other shade?*

The new neighbor, Joseph, word spread from a stack of misdelivered mail, worked at an accounting firm downtown. After his first week, the trim stayed red. *But not like blood*, Elaine thought as an edge of trim came into view through their bedroom window on Saturday while her husband moved inside her, behind her again, too rough. *It's not like blood at all*, she thought while she waited for Terry to make the sound that signaled an end to their morning "session." Guttural, desperate, maybe even a little resentful that her body, the exact dimensions of her hidden, blushed interior, triggered his pleasure. *Sometimes I am nothing but blood*, she thought as he rolled from her. Afterwards he always asked if she hurt, which to her sounded like, *Compliment my prowess and get those pancakes started.*

Elaine stood from the sheets. The remnants of their union left slow, thin trails down one thigh. She did not wipe away the mess. "I'm going to tell him to paint the trim."

"Who?" Her husband downloaded a book on his tablet, didn't look up.

"I'll tell him you know a guy. And you can make the pancakes today. I'm going for a run."

"But I don't know how to make pancakes?"

"Then order some."

"From where? Will they be cold when they get here?"

"Do you not like cold pancakes?"

"No one likes cold pancakes."

"I'm sure you'll figure it out."

Maybe Elaine wanted to run the rest of Terry from her body. She hated when he called them swimmers, those invisible nuisances hitching a ride inside her. Worse when he said, after each "coupling," her body was too old for worry.

Analyzing a lovemaking session afterwards, if you could even call it that, made Elaine feel more remorse. Perimenopause will do that to you. The few times, in the early years of marriage, one of her eggs and one of Terry's "swimmers" had tried to form something bigger than themselves, it had ended a few weeks after the pink positive mark on the pregnancy test. Destiny, and her aged eggs, promised not to bring a baby now.

Sometimes as she warmed up before a run, her legs still firm, her body feeling ten years younger in most places with each stretch, Elaine wondered if she and Terry had replaced their idea of an American dream with heritage pottery and half-drunken talks of future investment properties.

Pottery.

Pah-tah-ree.

Pot-teee-reeee.

Her heart beat faster than normal at the start of her run. Constriction in her calves alerted her to relax, slow her pace, not burn out so soon. She hit her feet, hard, against the neighborhood sidewalks in time to the schools of pottery she held in her head like names of children she would never have. Newcomb. Rockwood. Teco. Grueby. Who wants to be a middle-aged, or even a little past middle-aged, woman running in time to the names of vases? Couldn't she at least remember the names she picked for the children who stopped dividing their cells inside her? Or the names of the white paint meant to frame new Joseph's new-old door if he didn't like Spring Crème?

She ran faster to escape the image of the morning. The way he always asked her afterwards how she felt. As in, was there enough pleasure in the two-minute pornographic pumping I subjected you to? You don't really want to risk either of us touching you afterwards to emasculate me, right?

Right? White? White trim. Off-white. Harbor Haze. Whipping Cream. Adobe Hut. Greige. Grey beige, the new trend, house paint in seasonal palettes like makeup. Then black. The black van driven by a woman, she could see, moving slowly down a side street. Elaine thought she recognized her, before realizing she knew no women who drove vans. There was a friend the summer after high school graduation who drove a VW bus christened "Look Far" to a Dead show a few hours away. She couldn't remember what happened to the friend.

Elaine jogged past the house that was supposed to be her house to go hide in on nights when the oppressive feeling of neglect buzzed around her. A boom and a buzz and a boom-buzz-buzz in her ears as Terry marinated more salmon, no matter how much she protested, as she chopped a green apple to mix with the kale, the once or twice a week treat of a few spoonfuls of wild rice arranged on their plates like two pebbled paths to a longevity of more salmon and kale. And Terry was always right there, technically, when not at work. Chopping, walking her after dinner like the owners who trot around their purebred dogs after their own salmon meals.

Most of the time, after he told her about new clients, he asked about hers, which leaned more towards advising and less towards listening and, yes, she knew to bring in more money she must start listing the N. White and Company stoneware crocks on her site. But she still felt alone. More alone, even, than those nights she fell asleep listening to her Walkman in junior high, a few stuffed animals scattered around the room who had stopped comforting her years before, the soundtrack to some movie she hated about a school dance being banned, that everyone at school insisted she must love in order to fit in, droning through her dreams. Now Elaine jogged without any sound but her own heartbeat, her feet on the walk, up down, up down, her breath outwardly measured no matter how much she struggled to breathe, black van always either behind her or lodged, like a speck of grit, in the corner of one eye.

She passed the white house with the red trim, white and red like a starlight mint. *Do they even make those anymore?* Out front stood Joseph. Tall and dark, of course. Good-looking enough. After forty, any man in shape seemed good-looking enough to welcome to the neighborhood. Good-looking enough to criticize his terrible trim.

"I don't like it." Elaine pointed past his chestnut hair. She jogged in place. Joseph surveyed his new acquisition.

"I don't like any of it. It's just a place to stay, for now."

"What about the planters?"

"My wife did flowers. I don't do flowers."

He walked up the front steps and into the house without turning back. He did not introduce himself before shutting the front door.

Some people, Elaine thought as she jogged home. *Some people?* She sounded like her mother, who wasn't a person she ever wanted to sound like. Her breathing plateaued to a steady, effortless in, out, in, out, the way her lungs once worked at her college track meets. Jo-seph. Jo-seph. Jo-seph. *My feet. Listen to my feet, Jo-seph. I'm much too old for a crush. Is this a crush?* Jo. Jo. Jo. Seph. Seph. Seph. Almost the sound of a repetitive, resplendent yes. *And a crush on someone so flat, so uninteresting. A physical specimen, maybe, but divorced, and worse, bitter about it. Or maybe, worse yet, widowed?*

"I met him and he's horrible," Elaine yelled into the front room. Her body stiffened when she bent to untie her running shoes. "He doesn't like flowers." Terry never answered, no matter in what room he chose to spend his days off. "What kind of person doesn't like flowers?" she continued to question the empty spaces.

One hand beneath the band of her exercise bra drew

sweat away from her chest. She felt too much, then; too hot and too cold, too violated by the thought of living close to someone who didn't like flowers. *What's the point of making a living in the vase trade when each day fewer people arrange flowers?* Nothing more than empty vessels on a pretty shelf in a pretty house. A yellow house with off-white trim. Elaine, after all the years, had forgotten the names of the paint colors she and Terry picked out in their beginning.

The next morning she drank coffee, which tasted a little strange, in the nook off the L-shaped kitchen, her view a white piece of trim hanging over their guest bedroom.

"Someone left this for you on top of the mailbox." Terry handed Elaine a thin envelope.

Her name typed in the middle of the white expanse caused a pleasant, subtle shudder to overtake her body. Something interesting might finally happen. The six-lettered name, her name, known by someone other than herself and Terry. Of course it wasn't that unusual to find an envelope on top of the mailbox in their kind of neighborhood. She thought she almost knew everyone's names by now. One year, a few neighbors—Pamela, Susan, Heather?—exchanged Christmas cookies, though her morning jog, even through the winter snow, must be why she never received an invitation. Women her age, with salon-buttered highlights and thighs that don't touch, never receive invites to cookie exchanges. If a modern version of Tupperware parties existed—she vaguely remembered hearing the new thing was eating snacks at each other's houses while trying to sell candles—the other neighborhood women left out Elaine. No phone calls to help compile care packages on living room floors after each new American natural disaster, either, which was just as well, with all the near-priceless pottery claiming most flat spaces in her sitting area.

"It feels like a key to me," Terry said without looking up from his phone. Years ago he had mastered the art of scanning the daily news while walking around the house and yard.

Terry never keeps his hands off things that don't belong to him. My desk, my books, my mail, my body. Repulsion quaked Elaine as she imagined her husband leaving his fingerprints all over the house.

"It is a key." Her quick, smooth answer surprised her. "I told a woman down the street I'd check on her cats next week. She's going to, uhh, Mexico I think?"

"It's about time you made friends around here."

Terry, still reading the news, walked too close for her comfort to a Teco four-buttress vase. Elaine sensed some kind of imminent threat. Once the back door clicked shut, too loud and hard so early in the morning as Terry went to work, Elaine steadied the envelope under her desk lamp. Outside, a dark shadow moved past the front curtains.

There's no way the woman in the black van has that many errands.

Afraid the kitchen nook natural lighting might somehow belie the importance of whatever object hid inside the sealed surprise, Elaine opened the envelope at her desk. So careful, so slow, so close to the desk lamp her fingers flushed. She removed a piece of paper folded in thirds. Opening the paper revealed a starlight mint taped to the middle fold. The candy wrapper, yes the mint was wrapped, crinkled as she brought the paper closer.

Elaine folded the paper back in neat thirds, candy still attached. She hid the envelope in her desk under a pile of last year's auction house receipts. Having her own little secret warmed all of her. Even down there. Her cheeks tightened. Maybe she sat at her desk, smiling, the entire time she opened the envelope, which, as she pressed both hands on top of her receipts to make sure the mint still sat there, was not really a letter at all.

She pressed Terry's name on her phone. She pressed end before her husband answered. *I'm not obligated to tell him the only exciting thing that's happened to me in years. Plus, it's obvious who sent this to me.* Elaine wanted to call a friend before she remembered losing touch with most, no, with all of them over years of not returning calls or attending weddings or sending baby gifts. *It's okay, I'll just confront him myself. Him. Joseph. Nuisance. Neighbor. My handsome, quiet new neighbor. Handsome. Joseph.*

Casual but expensive clothes, a tan vicuna sweater imported without cruelty, fairly traded yoga pants, cherry red ballet flats for a little color, Elaine walked to the new neighbor's house. She left the red and white striped candy secure in her desk. A sugared pearl beneath all those papers glowing brighter by the minute.

Near his front steps Elaine noticed the missing flower baskets. She waited a long time after ringing the doorbell. Long enough for neighbors to drive by, for her to wave at the woman she thought she recognized the other day, again in the black van. The woman ignored her. Joseph opened the door dressed for work. His tie matched his shirt.

"I'm married." Elaine hid her hands in her too-long sweater sleeves. The weave itched her fingers.

"And?" The neighbor finished a cup of coffee, typed on his phone, stepped further out his front door to check the weather. He never stopped typing, one-thumbed.

"I appreciate you are new, but I thought you should know. And you really need to put your flowerboxes back up, or hang something from either side of the steps."

"Okay." The neighbor took a few steps back inside and shut the door.

Elaine stared at the peeling white paint. Overcome by the urge to leave a mark—*Why did you shut the door in my face? Did you just shut the door in my face?*—she removed one of her cherry red ballet flats and placed the shoe in front of Joseph's closed door.

Only one thing stuck in her head all those years after attending community college on a track scholarship. An English professor had taught that in the earliest known versions of Cinderella, she wore furry boots instead of glass slippers. In the approaching summer mid-morning heat, Elaine remembered the sexual sound of the words "furry boots." Cobbled from the soft white underbelly of a beautiful brown squirrel, the professor said. As she continued staring at her neighbor's front door, she imagined a very well-dressed woman losing a boot made of fur at a royal ball in the fairytale woods.

Pebbles stuck to her naked foot as she walked back to her house. The slight heel of her remaining shoe caused her legs to wobble at an uncomfortable angle until she abandoned the other shoe at the edge of another nameless neighbor's yard.

An afternoon sitting at her desk accomplished little. On her daily list of research prompts, the latest pottery pieces added to the market, the most ardent buyers, Elaine added notes about Cinderella and starlight mints. *I did tell Joseph his house looked like a giant peppermint candy, didn't I?* Marriage had floated Elaine out of the dating pool so many years ago, she had forgotten how to spot any potential wave moving towards her. Men did like to suck on hard candy more than women. She researched this earlier. Stronger orbicularis oris. More coffee and cigarettes. Those garlic pills that flush out cholesterol.

Again Elaine pushed on the papers lodged in her desk drawer. The sweet little bump waited, to be eaten or examined or thrown out, Elaine hadn't decided.

Throughout the evening, she checked for the mint after excusing herself from the dinner table to use the bathroom, or add more pepper to her salad, or answer the unheard beep of a text from her phone left in the other room. An intense wave of pleasure spread from the top of her head, right behind her ears, to the bottoms of her feet each time she felt for the mint. The all-knowing candy never let her down.

The next morning, Elaine awoke earlier than she had in years. Another envelope waited on the mailbox, this one a little damp on the back. *Freshly sealed*, she thought, *and I got to it before Terry.* He, or she, was still nearby. No, not she. The anonymous suitor must be a man. Only men with office jobs who move into new neighborhoods suck on peppermints; men who drink coffee all morning because no one stocked their cupboards or fridge. Whether or not Joseph refused to play the game of his own making yesterday didn't mean he was no player at all.

Without glancing around first, her shaking, eager fingers tore the edge of the envelope. No one bore witness to this illicit new game by her own sloppy luck, except those ubiquitous black vans she decided to get used to, yes, now more than one, maybe up to three, driving up and down her block but never slowing down near her house. Inside the envelope, without her name or any mark on the front, the same tri-folded piece of paper. The object, the size of another peppermint, almost landed in her front flower bed. Not taped, free to roam around its white field of paper, a starlight mint waited for her, not sticky, but also missing most of its stripe. Either sucked, or washed, until a pink shadow of its red swirl remained. The typed note on the paper read, "Put this in your mouth and think of me."

"How long have you been standing out here, hon?" Terry appeared, coffee cup in one hand. "You left to check the mail almost an hour ago."

"Are you sure I've been out here an hour?" Elaine's feet registered the cold. It was close to dangerously cold, standing barefooted in the dew-covered pansies. Petals stayed closed from last night's slumber.

"At least. What's in your mouth?"

Elaine obliged her husband and stuck out her tongue. The peppermint, sucked down to a flat, white disk the size of a pencil eraser, burned her taste buds. The tingle she recalled feeling upon first placing the candy in her mouth built into a tangible scorch.

Did I have some kind of spell, she thought as she swallowed the remains of the strange mint. *WebMD never listed this as a sign of perimenopause.*

In the first sincere statement to her husband in years, Elaine said, "I came to check the mail. Someone sent me a candy in an envelope, and I ate it."

Terry dropped his empty cup in the manicured grass beside her. He planted both hands on her shoulders with force. "You ate some goddamn piece of candy a weirdo sent you? What were you thinking? Go inside right now and make yourself throw up."

"Terry, baby," *When's the last time, or first time, I've ever called him Terry Baby?* "There's nothing to throw up." Again, she stuck out her tongue, felt the white, fur-like leftover mint coating, wondered if the whiteness of her tongue created another barrier between them.

"This isn't what I signed up for."

"Signed up for?"

"Give me whatever's in your hand, right now."

"Christ, Terry, it's just a piece of paper."

"Have you been cheating on me?" Terry grabbed the paper from Elaine's clamped fingers. He read the typed note to himself without comment before handing back the paper.

The pansies. Look at all the poor, smashed pansies.

Elaine stepped from her flower bed to consider stepping closer to her husband. Terry, bad in bed but good at providing. Beyond his salary, he knew when to bring her chocolate cake to quell her PMS, or a towel warm from the dryer on cold nights when she shook, wet, from the shower. No towel appeared now for her to wipe the dirt off her soles. No tea. No snack. Terry got in his car and drove towards work without looking at her. Elaine could not remember him ever not saying goodbye.

The mind builds thoughts into memories. Memories of new neighbors. Memories of mints. Memories of trying to get, and stay, clean. Warm water in the shower stung Elaine's toes. She bent to dislodge a splinter from her heel. *If Joseph had moved in last winter*, she thought, *this still would've happened. Snow shuts the whole town off from each other so long, all kinds of crazy things probably transpire. How many affairs are being consummated right now, while I wash, rinse and repeat?*

On top of her desk, in her front shirt pocket when she folded Terry's laundry, arranged hummus and crackers on a platter for her afternoon snack, her phone became a dark mirror that only reflected Elaine's distorted visage. No texts from Terry for hours, no matter how long she stared into the phone. An empty cracker plate balanced at the edge of her desk. She did not remember chewing or swallowing. She did not remember exactly what the typed sentence of the mystery paper said. She did not remember throwing the paper away.

Affairs must be exactly like this. Isn't there a phrase about the devil living in the beginning of things? The first ideas? The desires born of the gut over the mind before traveling to the brain in another married crisis of conscience?

The devil doesn't live in the details at all, Elaine thought. In her black screen her countenance looked young, alluring, even without lipstick or a good hair combing. In the phone screen, she looked the way she hoped. Terry ignoring her all afternoon helped release her real face. The face before the marriage and the miscarriages.

I'm still just a girl hoping a boy will notice me. Because Terry wasn't the first who did. Again Elaine marveled at the ease of her thoughts in organizing themselves into a justifiable triangle of what she instantly termed "affair logic." *Means he won't be the last. I need to prepare.*

When wives who don't stay at home wonder how wives who do spend their time, it's meted out in a complicated grid of chore versus pleasure. In the last hours before Terry arrived home, Elaine defrosted peas for dinner salads, shopped for a summer scarf online because she remembered reading an article at the dentist's office last week about the hottest new accessory. She allotted moments to checking her work email, plucking her eyebrows in a magnifying mirror. She found and sewed the missing button back on Terry's green plaid dress shirt, watched an episode of the show about the woman who makes everyone feel bad until they throw out all their junk. More hummus happened. On a whim, she downloaded a book of Russian fairytales with a cover of colorful nesting dolls. Elaine had always loved nesting dolls. She imagined each neighborhood as a set of dolls, and their houses, working in tandem, stacked together to not only function as a whole, but keep important secrets tucked at the center. Scanning her tablet, Elaine found the story *Zolushka*, the Russian Cinderella, but in this version she did not wear furry boots. How comfortable, through all of this, she felt not checking her phone.

"You left these on the porch."

Terry came home from work at the usual time. He threw Elaine's cherry red ballet flats into the foyer. They landed in a soft pile. Elaine dove towards the tile to inspect the shoes like two artifacts discovered on a suburban archeological dig.

She spoke to the shoes. "I don't know who sent me the letters."

"Letters?" Her husband glanced through a pile of junk mail he brought in with her shoes. "I have an idea."

Elaine assumed he meant Joseph. "I meant letter. Note, really. I guess the idea of a secret admirer excited me so much, I lost control a little."

"A little."

The slow, calculated movement of his finger past each piece of mail made the hair all over her body tingle. She hoped another letter did not wait for her, thrilling or not.

"Yes, just a little."

So this is what an affair does to a marriage, she thought. *Since I began deceiving Terry yesterday, I've never felt so honest. Right now, I feel like I can tell him almost anything.*

She lifted her shoes off the foyer tile by inserting each palm inside a ballet flat until she hit the inner sole. Her hands became two shiny red puppets. No cutesy actions lit her fingers as she stood in the foyer and stared at Terry as if her hands were always two red shoes.

"The way we have sex makes me feel bad," she said.

Her statement didn't hang in the air very long. With a married mercy Terry quickly asked, "How?" like he almost wanted to know the answer. The stack of mail quit moving in his hands.

"I'm not sure. It just does."

Terry set the junk mail on her desk. "Can we fix it, or is this a sign our time together is over?"

"Why would you say that?" Her hands sweated inside her shoes. She used the cracked edge of one shoe to brush a hair from her face.

"I think I'm still getting used to how this works."

"After all this time you expect me to believe you still don't know how our marriage works?"

"You're very different from anyone I've been with. I know it feels like we've been together forever, but there are always things to learn."

"About sex?"

"I guess?"

"I don't even remember who I was with before you. I can't believe you're bringing up old girlfriends from what feels like other lifetimes."

"I'm sorry. I feel like I'm messing this whole thing up. I'm just not used to all of this. And that's sexy, by the way." Terry pointed to the shoes, still on her hands. "Why don't you let me put them on your feet where they belong?"

The couple tried so hard, then, to stay a couple. Her husband's gesture filled Elaine with sorrow more than sensuality. She began to understand how much she wanted Joseph, or almost anyone except her husband, to bend down like Prince Charming and place her shoes on her feet.

Elaine sat on the coffee table, the risk of their mid-century modern table collapsing under her weight fueling her husband's fire. Terry sat on the couch. She let him swivel her thin body towards him. What would the woman in the TV show about decluttering do? That woman wasn't exactly sexy, not to other women, but Elaine knew how to find the hidden caches of porn on Terry's home computer. She knew what men thought they liked, which revealed infinitely more than what actually turned them on. She tilted her head a little, placed her calf in his lap.

"I believe you dropped these," he said in a voice deeper than his usual timbre.

"I was in a hurry to get home before my, uhh," she looked at Terry, he nodded in agreement, "husband knew I was missing." The shoe felt slick against her foot.

"Why were you in such a hurry?" Terry tickled her other foot by accident as he put on her shoe. Elaine didn't like the feeling. The word *gross* popped into her head.

"I'd never want to make my husband mad."

Husband.

Husband.

Not my husband.

Her eyes batted, an involuntary affliction. The word *husband*, mired now in affair logic, made her think of Joseph, or almost anyone besides Terry.

She fought through the roadblocks her brain threw in front of her. "So you have to promise to never tell him I'm with you right now."

In the bedroom, wearing only her cherry red ballet flats, Terry entered her from behind, this time bent over the bed so her feet touched the floor. Her arms splayed out in front of her on the dark sheets like light, twisting tentacles. Afterwards, Terry touched her and she pretended to enjoy his fingers while she wondered if the peas had thawed enough to sprinkle on their salads, if the squirrel of the fairytale forest sacrificed to make Cinderella's furry boots knew of his posthumous spot in history, if she had chosen expedited shipping for her summer scarf. At the five-minute mark she feigned the big, mostly elusive O, so her husband quit pretending not to be her husband.

"You're incredible," he said. With her eyes still closed she heard him get up to wash both of their bodies off his hands. "And crazy!" he yelled from the bathroom between too many pumps of soap.

Why is he always so quick to wash up after? And what about any of this makes me crazy?

Flowers arrived at the front door the next morning as they always did after a fight or a make-up. Predictable Terry, though Elaine guessed most men substituted red roses for apology. She had come to associate the color red with something more sad than celebratory.

The doorbell rang an hour after the flowers found a spot between two Greubys. A neighbor she didn't recognized handed Elaine a small card, much like the card that came with her flowers, down to the pink scalloped edges on view inside a peek-a-boo window.

"I didn't mean to snoop, but I saw your name." The woman looked a lot like Elaine except she did not wear ballet flats. On her belt hung a device that looked like an old-fashioned beeper. "It was stuck in my mail. I have no idea where it came from, but how would I. We may be a lot of things, but we aren't psychic."

"We as in women?" Both women watched a row of vans drive by. "Do you know what's up with so many people moving here recently?"

"Well, women like us. How are you adjusting? I'm not doing well this time around. I don't really like the neighborhood, or the man I'm with. And I can't help it but those vans give me the creeps every time."

"Me, too." Elaine grabbed the card. She did not apologize for her obvious curtness. "Not to sound rude, but I don't understand a lot of what you're talking about. You're being very personal."

"Sorry. It's a habit I've picked up. Some of us get that way."

"From living in the suburbs?"

"Sort of. A bunch of us get together every other Tuesday. You know, girls' night in. Wine, tapenade. We've been meaning to invite you. Just last Tuesday, Heather saw your lights on and almost walked over to get you, but we weren't sure you had the time."

Elaine left the nameless neighbor talking. She did not shut the front door as she turned to open her little card in the middle of her foyer, in private. She did not acknowledge, or care, if the neighbor kept talking, or stormed off, or slit her wrists on the front step. Elaine thought only of Joseph. Maybe not him, exactly. What she enjoyed more than discovering the new neighbor was finding someone new to consider, whether or not he spent any time considering her. The note, she determined as she fingered the curved edges, would excite her no matter who sent it.

The note said: Throw out the flowers. Don't make any excuses.

Who am I to not follow a direct order? I agreed to the rules. "For now," she said under her breath to the empty house, knowing no time limit loomed between her and the mystery admirer; knowing she had signed on for the duration.

A dozen long stems filled the trash can. Red petals, crushed at the bottom, covered the kitchen in a strong, sweet smell, almost like someone was cooking dessert.

Days went by without notes. Terry forgave her for the flowers after she swore she spotted two fat, juicy aphids on a stem. He took up a new habit of checking his phone dozens of times each evening. The couple's talks now focused on what to eat for dinner each night and how to cook it. A new knife showed up in the cupboard under the cutting board.

"To remove fish scales so we can start eating the skin, too," Terry said.

The word *skin* sounded foreign warbling around in his mouth. Sometimes he spoke of bones, a swollen ankle, a sore foot, or the way his muscles knitted back together after a hard workout in the gym, torn but hopefully a little bigger. Her husband never mentioned skin. Elaine read once that the favorite smell of all humans is the smell of skin, without any recollection of the smell of her husband beyond his deodorant, cologne, a slightly sticky product he brushed through his hair after showering.

She wondered what Joseph smelled like one night as Terry entered her body brusquely, a rare time he pressed his skin on top of hers. Reverting back to his old ways of no eye contact, and no foreplay, after the ballet flat incident, Elaine folded her thoughts deeper into herself while she waited for him to finish. Anytime she opened her eyes, she only saw Terry's chest. Not a bad chest, grey-haired, in some parts still dark, with no smell.

"Why don't you touch me anymore?" she asked in a break between thrusts.

"What?" Terry stopped to brush a hair off his forehead.

Elaine never felt much. An article in a women's magazine years ago made her question their "fit."

"When you first met me, you couldn't keep your fingers out of me." Her voice sounded breathy as the weight of Terry's body compressed her diaphragm.

He panted, slowed his rhythm. "I hate it when you talk like that."

"Like what?"

"Vulgar. I don't like it during sex. You know that's part of our rules."

"Since when do married people have rules? And if I

can't sound vulgar when you're fucking me, when can I?"

"Don't say that word." Terry broke contact from his wife's body. He rolled away from her. "You know I hate it when women say that word." He stood up and walked to the bathroom. "I've been very clear about that."

"Why don't you go wash up like you usually do and leave me alone, then?" Elaine yelled from bed.

She rose for water and a snack while Terry barricaded himself in the bathroom. She felt like she had spent over half of her marriage staring at that door.

"And we need to figure out something to eat besides hummus. I'm fucking sick of it," she swore at the closed expanse.

Elaine moved through the living room without turning on a light. *Like a big, sleek cat*, she thought, never bumping against one priceless vase. She craved sugar, a rare but distinct craving only sugar can cure.

"I'm not snacking because I'm depressed!" she shouted through the house as loud as she could. "I'm just hungry."

Two healthy, middle-aged people with enough money to reach old age, still healthy, meant the couple lived in a world void of snacks, even an energy bar forgotten in a back cupboard bought for a nature hike last summer. It was way too late in their small town to order take-out, and sometimes women of a certain age can only be satisfied with chocolate. The urge came three times as often as Elaine gave in to the indulgence, but that night, she needed the dark stuff.

Succumbing to the pointless ritual of checking every cupboard for a magic candy bar led Elaine to stand, empty stomached, in front of her double refrigerator doors. The only light in the house, besides the illicit white hush that enveloped her husband as much as it pushed itself under the crack in the bathroom door, hit her almost with a feeling of heat instead of cold as she opened the fridge to reveal a can of chocolate syrup and a can of whipped cream.

A small envelope sat propped against the whipped cream canister with a note inside, written in big block letters. "Shh. Don't tell . . . "

Opening the freezer divulged a pint of chocolate ice cream swirled with a ribbon of chocolate so dark, Elaine tilted the pint to her face to make sure someone hadn't mixed in a black velvet ribbon. The pint felt so cold in her palm. Weighted with chocolate syrup under one arm and whipping cream under the other, she walked off the front porch into a quiet night, barefoot and aimed towards Joseph. Houses up the hill shed golden husks of light onto her street, just enough for her eyes to focus as she walked.

On his front porch Elaine tiptoed towards a bench Joseph had arranged under one of the bay windows. What scene waited on the other side as Elaine dipped that first spoon into the perfectly melting brown puddle pooled at the top of the pint? Her tongue didn't register taste as much as the idea that another man fed her. Someone besides Terry who somehow, without ever saying a thing, expected her to genuflect before each nightly salmon offering as if he alone sustained her.

"Wouldn't it be better to eat this inside?" Elaine whispered to herself from the bench.

One click, absorbed into the quiet, and the front door opened with little resistance. She wiped her bare feet on a stiff rug laid over the entryway. She would never place a rug there in her dream house. Instinctively, she stepped left into the living room, dark except for a blue dot of light from the television cable box. As her eyes adapted to the neon blue iris, the all-knowing oracle guiding her towards a window box, the cold outside bench belonged now to someone on the other side of this warm inner sanctum.

The warmth gave way to the coolness of something running down the length of her arm before Elaine realized she had tilted the ice cream to the point of spilling. She often felt this way. Too many thoughts, and remembered promises, and forgotten dreams mixed themselves with the chores list always floating in front of her, took precedence over paying attention to where her body came to light in the world. *Always one step ahead or behind, my blood, my bones, my heart, my Joseph.*

Elaine managed to clean up the mess with a kitchen towel before letting herself out. If Joseph was home, she never knew as she left the discards of her impromptu ice cream social melting on his front porch. A woman like her, with a noticeable thigh gap, sucking down most of a can of whipped cream to nothing, when left behind, but a thank you.

"Fucking kids!" Terry hollered from the front porch early the next morning. He carried the empty whipped cream canister, pint and a dirty spoon on the morning paper he arranged into a flimsy tray. "This neighborhood's going to shit."

"Where did you get all of that?" Elaine sipped her morning coffee at her desk. Terry called the flavor Almond Joy. He added coconut syrup to both drinks each day. "And I hate my coffee."

"What's wrong with it?" Terry filled the kitchen trash with Elaine's sticky secrets.

"Why can't I just have it the way I like it, black with one sugar?"

"Because this is the first time you've said you don't like it."

"That's not true." She slammed the mug a little too hard against the desk. "I tell you every morning how much I hate it. I've been telling you for years."

"Listen, I've only known you a week. I don't know what your deal is, but I'm paying a lot for your service, and each day you're shittier than you were the day before. Can't you ease up a little?"

"Terry, you sound completely insane."

"Jesus, either get your head all the way in the game or you might as well go."

"Go where?"

"Wherever you came from."

"What are you talking about?"

A feeling of someone standing behind her, though no one stood anywhere near, crept over Elaine. Turning, she saw nothing but the room full of vases, each sitting on their own assigned shelf almost like rows of schoolchildren ready to start their day.

She gestured towards the pottery. "If this isn't where I'm supposed to be, how come I know so much about all of them?"

"I spent the extra hundred bucks and ordered the dossier for a more authentic experience. It's probably somewhere in my desk."

"This is my desk?" Elaine cursed herself in her head as her disoriented voice made her words sound so tenable. "I meant, this is my desk. This is where I buy and sell vases while you work downtown."

Terry poured another coconut stream into his coffee. Elaine wondered how the drink stayed warm with so much cold syrup.

"Downtown doing what?" he asked.

"Don't be stupid."

She squirreled her hands through the contents of each

desk drawer. Unfamiliar papers filled the spaces. Formulas and numbers, like the code to a foreign language she did not understand how to decipher. He poured in one more syrup shot, smiled as he gulped the coconut caffeine.

"Come on, what do I do for a living?"

Elaine, at her desk filled with strange, what she now saw as dangerous, papers, had no idea. "If you really are paying me to participate in some kind of game, you don't seem very happy with the outcome. And I still think you sound crazy."

"That's the game I signed up for."

"What's it called, then, this game you supposedly paid good money for?" She didn't feel even half as dizzy as she expected.

"Work's been really busy so I haven't had time to get out and meet anyone. The package I ordered is called Pretend Wife."

Elaine gasped, audibly. *Like in some overly dramatic movie*, she thought. Pretend Wife. Am I really playing the part of Terry's Pretend Wife?

What did it mean, anyway, to be, or pretend to be, a wife? Not sleeping with anyone else, definitely not having sex with another man the rest of your life. Maybe even a good wife found herself in bed with another woman, once every five or ten years as part of an anniversary present, but only if the husband at the very least watched, and the women had nothing in common but existing as women in a suburban swinger fantasy. Most wives don't do this. At a certain point in the life of a marriage, most wives no longer have sex, at least not with any regularity or voraciousness. Does this mean they are no longer wives?

"Are you playing Pretending Husband?"

"I am pretending, but this mostly falls on you. You're the expert."

Elaine knocked over her coffee cup with a tense, errant elbow. The brown liquid, faintly smelling of sunscreen, a memory of a beach long ago, if it was even a real memory, flooded Terry's desk.

"But I feel like we've been together for years?"

"Because you're one of the best service providers in the state. The reviews say you put your heart in it, every time." He examined his wet, stained desk. "Spills and breakage will be deducted from your final bill, of course."

When Elaine scanned the room, everything looked familiar the way a hotel room looks familiar after the first night. She knew Terry kept a blue toothbrush in a white cup in the bathroom. That cup sat, and would be sitting, on the sink because she had seen the cup sitting there every time she entered the bathroom the past week. The more she ran the image of the white cup through her mind, though, she could not remember where the object came from. Or the toothbrush. And why did her pink toothbrush look so new to her? A few times over the past days she had noticed how the bristles, not quote broken in, scraped her gums and tongue. She found no cup for her toothbrush. When she stood the brush next to Terry's each night, blue bristles touching pink bristles in the same white cup, by morning the pink brush laid on its side by the sink, abandoned.

Naked, she thought, *vulnerable without its own space.* The pink color reminded her more of a girl's toothbrush than something a woman had picked out. Maybe the game manager provided toiletries?

"Did you buy my toothbrush?" Elaine asked through the closed bathroom door. *Was her name even Elaine?*

"You must've picked one out of the drawer. I keep extras for the providers. Do you like it?"

"Before this morning I did, very much."

Terry, now a stranger, emerged from the bathroom wearing a button-down shirt and slacks.

"You're very good at what you do. You've made me feel a combination of domesticity tinged with regret mixed with passionless sex. Now I know I made the right choice staying single. I'll never be able to thank you enough."

"Thank me?"

"But you need to get to your next appointment now, remember? I know it's not what you usually do, but I appreciate you agreeing to split your fee between Joseph and me."

The strange man's large hand gripped the pink toothbrush. The gesture, and its color, now looked obscene. A feeling of nausea rose in Elaine.

"I guess we won't be needing this anymore. I read somewhere that single men prefer women's mouths to smell like beer. Married men prefer toothpaste. Isn't that wild?"

"Toothpaste. I guess that makes sense. But I don't remember anything about my next appointment. You know Joseph?"

"We work in the same building downtown. I know it's unorthodox, but your company charges so much, we needed to split our time to afford you. And believe me, it was worth it. I'm sure he agrees. Just let yourself out after you gather your things. After all," he winked in an exaggerated, cartoonish way that made him look like a child, "you are my wife."

Terry tossed the pink toothbrush in the bathroom trash on the way out. Elaine returned a few moments after he drove away to make sure the brush still sat at the top of a can of wadded tissues and used tampons. She unwrapped a tampon from its swaddle of Kleenex. The cotton fluff looked as white as when she removed it from the plastic tube days earlier. No blood had darkened and browned to that strong-smelling monthly rust on any of the other "used" tampons she unwrapped for inspection.

"Was part of the game pretending to be on my period? The only thing red in this neighborhood," she spoke to the bathroom mirror, "is that neighbor's horrible trim."

Red, not pink. Not just my neighbor, home. My home. Home?

Elaine packed a bag of what started to look like someone else's clothes. *Game clothes*, she thought, *not my clothes*. She decided to leave everything that belonged to her, rented, no doubt, one week at a time, and go home to Joseph with nothing but her pajamas and her red shoes. Terry was a liar. She understood everything now.

Elaine walked into the house without knocking.

"You're not supposed to be here until tomorrow." Joseph kept reading the news on a laptop centered in the middle of the kitchen table. "I can't afford an extra day."

Ignoring him, she struggled to find a pan in the large kitchen and something to fry. Where was the oil, the salt? It was such a shame they both worked too much to compose even a modest pantry. "I should've stocked up before last week. We're out of everything again."

"I didn't order the wife game. Aren't you ID40-S? Can I adjust the charges before I pay. I hate trying to get a rep on the phone."

Elaine left the empty pan on the stove, the blue insistence of gas flame heating up nothing. In the bathroom off the kitchen, she guessed the correct door after one wrong try, she stared at photographs of Joseph with a blonde woman in places she had never visited. The words *Machu Picchu* came to mind as her eyes studied a pyramid ruin carved with innumerable stairs in the middle of a jungle. She only knew the name of the Peruvian citadel because of a junior high geography class. An entire unit devoted to the Incas and their quipu, the necklace of knotted "talking strings" her clumsy hands could not loop with even the larger beads without the teacher's help. The teacher with the unusual first name, Zander, who went by Mr. Zander, who made a big deal in class about helping Elaine like no student ever needed help before. He pointed out to the others Elaine's complete lack of coordination.

The school counselor offered her a red Lifesaver after she complained about Mr. Zander embarrassing her in front of everyone. He explained in his overly soft, overly concerned voice that it was her job to let herself be embarrassed for the greater good of helping Mr. Zander feel like an accomplished teacher. It was her lot in life, this time around, he whispered, to provide for others. To provide, mostly, for men.

"Provide for men?"

"Boys first, but the men will follow. There are many more girls in the world just like you, but no other young providers in this district or the next two over. You can't tell anyone I told you this, especially not your parents."

Elaine went home from school that afternoon with a candy red tongue. She never ate another Lifesaver again, didn't understand anything the counselor said, blocked it all from her mind until she stood, staring, at the blonde woman in the photo. She did remember that she and the counselor sat on his office carpet, cross legged and with their knees almost touching, like they were in on a catastrophic secret, and how Saint Zander never helped her tie another bead onto her mess of embroidery floss. Her mother never found time to help the way Joseph had never found time between clients to listen to her story about the knots. Or he would tell her she spoke in knots, his term for stories that never, in his analytical, tie-always-matching-his-shirt approach to life, came to a climax. She resented the blonde woman in the photos. She resented the Incas and their series of complicated knots. Joseph followed her into the bathroom.

"And I didn't sign up for tears. Once Marion left, the service promised no tears."

Elaine removed the cherry red ballet flats. She handed the shoes to Joseph and sat on the closed toilet seat. He handed them back before asking Elaine to come by tomorrow.

"I'll be less distracted when you're actually supposed to be here."

"I really don't belong here, either?"

Outside, the red trim relished its redness. Down the street, who knows what happened to all those vases.

"The thing is you do, but only as an admirer. That's the package I paid for. Just a little adoration. The service promised this would help me move past the divorce."

The overstuffed couch felt too soft as it curled around Elaine's body once she sulked out of the bathroom to head for the nearest perch. "I thought we lived here, together? Terry down the street made it sound like—"

Joseph pushed up his shirt sleeves, pointed in the direction of what Elaine thought was her home. "Terry knows vases, not women. I've been his accountant for years." He pushed the knob on a French press while Elaine imagined swirling about the bottom of the glass carafe, a lost speck in a thousand. "I never should've given him a gift certificate for Christmas. I certainly never thought he'd ask to share a game, even with his inherent cheapness. Games are never allowed to overlap, and now I see why. It's not very fair to either of us, or to you."

Elaine waited for him to offer her a cup of coffee. He didn't. "Me?"

"I can't imagine what this puts you through in the course of a lifetime. Not like you have any choice, but it still must be a colossal mindfuck, what you do."

"I don't understand."

"I'd tell you to go ask one of your friends to explain it, but their memories get erased after each session, too. They can't help any better than I can, but I'll give it a quick try."

He pulled up a contract on his computer. Elaine thought of asking him for a boiled egg. She assumed fit men ate boiled eggs.

"See," Joseph pointed to a grid, "tomorrow is our

designated time."

"Yes, I understand." Elaine scanned the grid. She pretended to grasp the meaning of a checked box with tomorrow's date, 3pm, along with a list of what she agreed to provide, only her first name signed at the bottom of the bond.

Complain about red trim and lack of flower baskets, check.

Show up dressed in designer yoga pants, check. Sneak in to eat ice cream in the living room.

Send yourself anonymous notes from me.

Include candy.

Make them good.

Everything, in bold letters, Elaine had agreed to provide. "So even the notes were part of this?"

"The notes were the biggest part, and the only way Terry and I could figure out how to share your service for a week without you catching on. I'm sorry we were so deceptive but it's been drummed into all of us since elementary school that providers aren't real."

"You don't think I'm real?"

"They train us in school to see you as not quite human. You're more like a tool. A very pretty, very desirable tool."

"Who wouldn't want to be a pretty, desirable tool?" Elaine said with a hint of cynicism she assumed would count against her when it came time for both Terry and Joseph to pay.

"You can't really blame me. All men are taught from practically birth to never fall in love or settle down with a provider. I doubt your boss would let you, anyway."

Elaine thought about the notes, why they meant so much to her, how they felt like they belonged to her since, she now realized, nothing else did.

"How long will it take me to forget my previous assignment?"

"I've never asked a provider anything personal. I wouldn't dare."

"How many have you seen?"

She wished the contract was printed instead of virtual. She longed for some piece of evidence about her, with her name, whether or not it was really her name, that she could hold in her hands, run her fingers across; something to connect her to all of this.

"I hired quite a few before my marriage. After, not many. I would say you're definitely the best at what you do, if it's any solace."

Joseph clicked away the contract from his laptop screen. Elaine felt like he wanted her to leave. She exited the front door without saying anything, finally admitting to herself, as she walked down the street and past Terry's house, that her shoes hurt. The color, the cut, the style. Elaine hated everything about the red ballet flats, especially the way they pinched her toes and gouged the backs of her heels. Since she could not remember the gaps between jobs, she had no idea where the shoes even came from, but they hurt, bad.

"My feet hurt," she said out loud. She stopped in the middle of the street. "And I hate kale, and grilled salmon, and coconut syrup in my coffee, and pink toothbrushes, and never being able to make my own decisions, about anything." Elaine bent as close as she could to her feet. "You are hurting me," she said to the shiny red shoes.

Neighbors on either side of the street went about the business of being neighbors. A black van pulled up next to her. The woman who had visited Terry's house to give Elaine the card with her name on it got into the van while another woman stepped out. The woman exiting the van looked a little like Elaine, but mostly nothing like her. While Elaine watched, the woman walked towards Terry's house, a little disoriented. She opened the front door without knocking and shut the door behind her.

Another van pulled up close to Elaine. Two women sat in front.

"ID40-S," the woman in the passenger seat spoke to Elaine, "it's time. We've heard great feedback. Your next assignment is ready."

The passenger, an average-looking, middle-aged blonde woman who looked more like a receptionist at a law firm, motioned for her to get in back. Elaine shook her head no. Before the van doors opened, she took off running, first down the middle of the street before throwing off her shoes to run, fast and barefoot, across neighboring lawn after lawn. She leapt over short fences, scrambled up taller ones, trampled every flowerbed in her path. She never looked back to see if the van followed her.

Elaine ran until she forgot why she was running. She ran until she realized she didn't know her own name. She ran until the landscaped lawns turned into empty lots, then long swaths of golden meadowland. Elaine ran until it didn't matter if she had a name, a place to be, an identity past the next beat of her heart and the next pound of her foot.

She ran for a very long time.

ACKNOWLEDGMENTS

Three of the *Four Views*, in slightly different form, appeared in *Back Scat Review #8—Seduction*.

Four Views, in a slightly different form, was named a finalist for the Conium Review 2018 Innovative Short Fiction Contest, and appeared in *The Conium Review*.

The Keeper of the Waldeinsamkeit was named a runner-up for the 2019 Calvino Prize.

The Keeper of the Waldeinsamkeit also appeared, in a shortened form, in the surreal novella *Sweet and Vicious*, published by Black Scat Books.

ABOUT THE AUTHOR

SUZANNE BURNS writes both poetry and fiction. Her last short story collection, *The Veneration of Monsters*, was named a Top 100 Fiction Book of the Year by Kirkus Reviews. She is currently working on a new novel.

www.ingramcontent.com/pod-product-compliance
Lightning Source LLC
Chambersburg PA
CBHW031020160726
47991CB00005B/1803